Miami Noir 1987

James J. Caterino

Other published works by James J. Caterino include

Pop Culture Musings and Other Stuff
Jennifer the Sketchbook Girl
Fantastic Stories: Season 2
The Mesomorph
Femme Fatales: The Art of James J, Caterino
The Green Girl
Super Hornet 1942
Sketchbook 5: The Art of James J. Caterino
The Girl from the Stars
Watch the Skies

Chapter 1 – Miami

March 1st, 1987, was when it all began. That date is the most important in my existence. That was the day I became truly alive. Because that was the day I met Valerie.

It's hard to properly verbalize that effect she had on me that very first moment I gazed upon her golden, sunlit locks during the backyard pool party at 1313 Tiger Tail Lane in the heart of the Coconut Grove section of Miami.

Since I am a filmmaker, I can best describe it in cinematic terms.

I walked out onto the patio/pool area of my cousin's backyard. It was a lush setting of greens and pastels where she often held these Saturday and Sunday afternoon get-togethers, festive events that looked and felt like casting parties for an episode of *Miami Vice*.

A Reggae tune was jamming, adding to the tropical feel. I scanned around, and that's when I saw her.

She was standing on the other side of the pool, holding a drink with a hand so exquisitely shaped and with nails so perfectly manicured, I concluded that she must be a hand model.

I noticed her pretending like she was listening to some rambling dope chirping her ear off about something that must have been absolutely excruciating to listen to.

Then my eyes locked onto her as I took in her insanely perfect, statuesque form, clad in a perfectly fitted tan-colored dress.

She was a statuesque, formidable presence, as elegant and classy as the most elite Paris runway model you could ever imagine. But she was certainly no stick figure. She was athletic with toned muscles, but not bodybuilder, Gold's Gym type muscles. More like a tennis player or a dancer. They were long and lean muscles that I could see in the arm that was holding the drink and in her ridiculous, perfectly formed sun-kissed bare legs that went on forever, until they ended in a pair of superbly formed and perfectly pedicured feet in a pair of shoes that seemed designed to show them off. Maybe she was a foot model too.

I was lost in the moment, staring at her with wonder, lust and savage desire when she busted me. Not with a glare, or even an uncomfortable or awkward gaze back. Instead, she answered my reflexive drooling with a soul-stirring smile—a piercing, life-altering smile that I could feel electrifying me from clear across the patio.

Then, we locked eyes—her crayon blues honed in on my obsessive gaze—and then it happened.

It was like I was suddenly living inside a movie, and this was the big moment. The money shot where the director gets to show off and pull a zoom/dolly—that disorienting cinematic move where the character and the background appear to move in opposite directions. It was as if she was now standing right in front of me, even though she was clear across the patio, standing on the other side of the pool.

I was blown away.

Nothing had ever had this kind of effect on me before. Movies sometimes, maybe. But certainly not a person. I knew I should immediately cross over to the other side of the patio and introduce myself to this living Goddess.

But I could not do that just yet. Because I was too excited. Literally excited. Yeah, in that way. So I had to calm down first to avoid any embarrassment. After all, this was a pool party, and I was in a pretty skimpy pair of denim shorts and a short sleeve silky tropical type dress shirt. So I took a walk around the house—which was not just my cousin's, but also my current and temporary place of residence. I had a cold drink of Orange Crush to try and calm my wanton lust.

Then I was able to slowly make my way back out to the patio for a proper introduction, just as she was walking inside. We crossed paths in the tight space of a narrow hallway, our bodies nearly touching. The sheer physical intensity of the encounter was almost too much to bear.

She had been radioactive from across the patio. But up close and personal, she was positively supernova. Just the tingling pleasure I felt from the touch her skin during her handshake was enough to make me want her more than I had wanted anyone or anything in my life. And her smell—all of her smells drew me in. Alluring but never over-bearing, her scents were, like the rest of her—that over-used word of perfection The smell of her skin, hair, and even breath—especially her breath—were absolutely intoxicating.

So in my inebriated state—drunk, not from alcohol, but from this insane vision simmering before me—I said as my opening line what should have been a closer uttered hours, if not days later.

"Would you like to be in my movie?" I asked.

She gave me a tilt of her head and a look that said she was, at the very least, curious.

"That depends," she said, leaning in closer to me, using her height to dominate me and her seductive breath to render me powerless.

"That depends," she repeated in a whisper, leaning in so close it took every bit if my quickly vanishing self-control to not kiss her.

"Depends on what?" I managed to say with a dry throat.

"What's the movie about?" she asked.

"You want the elevator pitch? Or the full-fledged in the head of the studio's office presentation?" I asked.

"Am I to be the lead in this movie?" she asked.

"Oh, you bet you are," I said.

"Then give me the full treatment," she purred. "I want to know what I'm signing up for."

I mentally queued up my big pitch and went for it.

"Picture this…" I formed my hands into a director's movie frame as I dramatically gestured and went into my pitch.

"We open on Biscayne Bay. The title card reads June 1977. We move down onto the beach and push in on a group of teenagers having a big get together, celebrating their graduation from high school. One of them has a boat, and they take turns going out onto the bay to water ski behind the boat.”

“We push in for a close-up of one of the couples, Jimmy and Amanda. We can tell they aren’t just high school sweethearts. This is true love. They literally have to pull themselves off of each other when they hear Amanda’s name being called. It is her turn to water ski.”

I paused for a second just to make sure she was with me. She was hanging on my every word. I went on with my pitch.

“We watch from Jimmy’s point of view on the beach as Amanda zips by from out on the bay, jumping over the wake of the boat, dipping and twisting. She is quite good at water skiing and having a blast. Everybody is watching her, including the driver of the boat. He does not notice what we see—another boat heading right at them, moving erratically. The other boat is packed with people, blasting music—a party boat. Amanda tries to scream to warn the driver about the approaching party boat. Finally, he does turn around, tries to swerve, but it’s too late. There is a violent collision. A huge fireball explosion. And afterward, no sign of Amanda. Only her abandoned, water skies.”

“Oh shit,” she gasped. “Then what happens?”

“We fade to black, title card—10 years later. We open on a man, a very ordinary man, staring down at the sidewalk street from the window of his office on Biscayne Boulevard. We move in for a close-up on him, and we see it’s Jimmy. Ten years older. He looks dull. Beaten. The sparkle from his eyes gone.”

I continued.

“His vision zooms in on a beautiful woman walking on the sidewalk below who catches his eye. He scrambles to leave his office, announcing he is heading out for lunch.”

“Cut to Jimmy walking about in downtown Coconut Grove.—a voyeur—obsessively pursuing this beautiful woman. There is something about her. Something he is powerfully drawn to. Something so familiar.

"He continues to pursue her, doing his best to act nonchalant, getting a cup of coffee, perusing the window of a bookstore until—he see finally see her up close. And she looks just like her. Just like Amanda. His lost love who died ten years earlier."

I had done a few pitches to producers who came by our directing class, so I had a good feel for how it was going. And I knew she was all in, wide-eyed in anticipation of what came next.

"But how?" she asked.

"Exactly," I said. "It's impossible."

"I mean, it can't be, right?" I said. "He saw her die. But she looks just like her. He is spellbound and begins to follow her closer, tracking her throughout downtown and into the Plaza and into the AMC Theater. He even goes into the theater where she is watching a movie and takes a seat a few rows behind her. And as the final credits roll, continues his pursuit. Then, outside the theater, at long last, as she stops and turns, pivoting around to face her pursuer, and…"

I stopped cold and gave her a deliberate, torturous cliff-hanger pause.

"And then what?" she asked, with urgent anticipation.

"I can't give it all away now, can I?" he asked. "Not before we've even had our first date."

She didn't slap me or walk away. So I took that as a good sign.

"You tease," she said. "And I don't even know your name Mister Movie Producer."

"Bite your tongue. I'm a director," I said. "Rem. Rem Rasso."

"I'm Valerie. Valerie Perry," she said, shaking my hand again.

This time she held onto it, and ever so gently caressed the inside of my palm with her fingertips. I thought I was going to die from the quaking spasm of pleasure it caused.

"And Rem Rasso sounds like a made-up stage name," she said. "What is that? Like, your director's name?"

"Indeed. But it's my real name too," I said. "You can even ask our host over there. She's my cousin."

I motioned over to Sheila, who was standing down the hall, passing out slivers of cake.

She nodded and smiled as if impressed.

"So far, so good, Rem," she said. "But if I'm going to sign on board to such a lurid and mysterious film, I'd need to know who is playing the lead male first."

I just gave her a look, smiled, and nodded.

"Jack of all trades, huh, Rem?" she said.

"Not really. I just come cheap," I said. "Plus, I want to save the bulk of the budget to get the right lead actress. She will make or break this film. And if it's you…well, let's just say I feel really good about this movie's chances at the Coconut Grove film festival this summer."

She looked me up and down, then locked onto my eyes. I could tell that she was not just playing now. She was taking me seriously.

She leaned in and whispered into my ear.

"Consider me intrigued, Rem Rasso," she whispered.

Then she kissed me on the cheek, excused herself for what I presumed was the restroom. But as she walked away, I saw her check the time on the Rolex on her left wrist and head out the front door.

I followed in an obsessive panic, feeling like Jimmy from my own script, cringing at the thought of not ever seeing her again.

I opened the front door to see her standing on the side of the street just as a snazzy-looking white BMW convertible motored up to the curb.

"Valerie, wait," I called out.

She smiled and waved.

"Your cousin has my number," she said. "Call me."

She waved again, then climbed down into the passenger seat of the BMW. I could now get a good look at the driver. He was spiffily dressed. A slick Mafioso type. What my Italian friends and relatives back in Pittsburgh would call a "guinea bastard." Probably named Tony or Joey. Something about the way they interacted told me that he was not her boyfriend—thank God. He seemed more like her driver, or even bodyguard.

Whoever this Valerie was, all I knew was I needed more of her.

As the white BMW sped away up the road toward U.S. 1, all I could think about was seeing her again.

Chapter 2 – The Return of Amanda

The thing about asking her to be in my movie—that was real.

Yeah, sure, it was a line. And I would have used any, and every line imaginable to a have a chance to be anywhere near this magnificent creature named Valerie. But the movie was real, or at least I was busting my ass to try and make it real.

The name of this great opus in the making was called *The Return of Amanda.*

It was all about the movie—everything I did.

That was the real reason I had come to Miami. Not to get a "real job" after college like I had told my parents and everybody up north. I was here because I wanted to be the next movie brat director. And *The Return of Amanda* was to be my calling card, the way *Amblin* was for Steven Spielberg, or *Home Movies* was for Brian De Palma.

Growing up in the late 1970s and early 80s in Pittsburgh, Pennsylvania, movie directors were my rock stars—my celebrity athletes.

The pictures on the wall of my childhood bedroom were one sheet film posters that stood above the stacks of movie magazines such as *Starlog* and *Cinefantastique* that were neatly stacked on the floor upon row after row, right next to my Super 8 film camera and a box full of homemade lighting equipment.

It was passion, to be sure, but upon reaching that age where you need to decide what the hell you are going to do with your life so you can eat and have a roof over your head, such passions must be downgraded into the categories of hobbies or even merely interests.

This was especially true in the down to earth/work for a living blue collar world of Western Pennsylvania circa 1982, the year of my high school graduation. In my case, even more so, because I was lucky enough to nab a football scholarship to Pitt. Lucky being the operative word. A recruiter there was best friends with my high school linebacker coach, saw me play a few games in high school, and took a shine to me. But at five feet ten, two hundred twenty pounds (but that's juiced up in offseason pre-camp. My actual playing weight was two-hundred soaking wet), I was a long shot to last long at Pitt, let alone ever have any prospects beyond that.

I was warned by everybody and their brother to not waste this God-given lucky break by dicking around with "those artsy-fartsy basket weaving classes" and to prepare for a career in the business world. Of course, I had a major hard-on for film, but this was Pitt, not USC or UCLA. There was no such as a major, or even a minor, in film. So I went with the program, got a degree in economics, but used every single elective I had available to take any and every film or movie-related course available at the school.

With job prospects of any kind looking dim in the city at the time, I came to Miami under the guise that I was here to get a "real" job, and maybe take a class or two at the University of Miami, eventually working toward an MBA.

The thought of that made we want to run down to the Biscayne Bay Bridge and jump. So I went another route.

I was working at a Coral Gables muscle head gym called Hard Bodies, taking a directing class at UM, and prepping to make the film that would not only be my class project for the final exam, but would be my entry at the Coconut Grove Film Festival, and my ticket to the stars. Then I could get out of Sheila's hair, get my own place and gig, and work on becoming the next movie brat success story.

I had it all planned out, and it all depended on my film, *The Return of Amanda*. And the success of that film all depended on the lead actress. Now, with Valerie, I had found her. I just had to close the deal.

Oh, there was one other problem. Money.

Even small indie flicks cost money to make. People like to get paid and fed. Locations need to be secured. Permits obtained. Sets need to be dressed. Wardrobes purchased. Cameras and lights rented. Film edited and processed. And I wanted my movie to look and sound fantastic, so I refused to go cheap when it came to cinematography and music. So yeah, I needed money.

But first, I needed to make sure I had Valerie. If I could just get her, somehow, I thought the money would come too.

Chapter 3 – Date with a Goddess

Before I approached my cousin, Sheila, for the scoop on Valerie, I was able to butter her up with some good news I received.

One of my gym buddies at Hard Bodies, Bobby Z, probably my best friend since moving here to Miami, called to tell me his roommate got engaged and was bailing on him. He lived at a high rise apartment complex called Summer Winds that sat just off I-95 at 163rd Street in North Miami. It was still close enough to the gym to make it work, and my share of the rent would be two twenty-five plus half the electric and phone. With my piker salary from the gym, it would be a tight squeeze, but doable.

I thanked Sheila profusely for putting my ass up, telling her she could now have her privacy back.

"Damn, I actually prefer having you around, cousin," she said. "You're quiet, organized, and a neat freak. The place has never been so clean."

"There is one more thing I need to ask from you," I said. "It's about a girl I met at the party here yesterday. Well, not a girl. Wrong word. This was a woman. A woman if there ever was one."

Sheila looked at me with saucer eyes conveying shock, surprise—and worry.

"Damn, you just met the chick and are sounding all smitten," she said. "What's with that?"

I just shrugged my shoulders.

Sheila did indeed have Valerie's contact information. But she issued it to me with an ominous warning.

"Oh, I get why you are so into her. She's a hot number. A real four-alarm fire," Shelia said. "Just proceed with caution."

"Oh?" I asked.

"Well, you know how I had that sweet acting gig on *Miami Vice* and how you love parking in front of the TV every Friday night, never missing an episode?" she asked.

"Yeah?" I said.

"Let's just say, based on some of the characters I've seen Valerie hanging out with, her life is like an actual real-life *Miami Vice*," Shelia said.

I nodded and smiled. Shelia knew me well enough to know why.

"That was supposed to warn you away, not turn you on," she said.

"I think you picked the wrong analogy for that effect," I said.

"Yeah, I guess so," she said. "Really. Just be careful, cousin. These people don't play."

"No worries, cousin," I said. "I'm not looking to get mixed up in any Miami gangster shit. Just to get Valerie to star in my movie."

She rolled her eyes. Though she never said it aloud, I was sure she thought the movie was a foolish pipe dream.

She turned and went back into a drawer behind her and pulled a wad of twenty-dollar bills. She grabbed my wrist and slapped the bills into my hand.

"Hey, that's bullshit. I should be the one handing you money," I protested.

"Well, you will be handing me money when you pay me back," she said. "In the meantime, there's two-hundred bucks there. I don't want you embarrassing me out there. So take her somewhere nice."

"Thanks, cousin. I really appreciate it," I said. "You won't regret this."

"I know," she said. "Just make sure that you don't."

Valerie sounded surprised and downright enthusiastic to hear from me in a shy, smitten, school girl kind of way. Which seemed out of character, but only added more rocket fuel to the already burning fire I had for her.

"Pick me up Friday night at seven. I'll take care of the plans," she said, sounding much more like the take the charge alpha female I had met at the party. This, too, was something I found attractive. Truth be told, pretty much everything about her turned me on. God, help me.

The date was all set. So I spent my week working at Hard Bodies by day, and gradually moving my limited amount of stuff into the apartment at Summer Winds during the evenings and polishing up my *The Return of Amanda* script, as I counted down the hours until Friday Night while OCD-ing over what the hell I was going to wear.

I opted for a white blue pastel pair of loose slacks, a short-sleeve collared clingy black silk shirt, and a pair of white slip-on flat suede boat shoes. To top off my grooming, I caked half a bottle of LA Look gel onto my kinky, frizzy locks, to slick back my hair. In other words, I was a walking exaggeration of "Miami 80's character". A Guido in the tropics.

I was to pick her up at her Adventura apartment, which was only a few miles from my new pad at Summer Winds in North Miami with Johnny Z. But those few miles made all the difference in the world. Summer Winds was a decent, nice looking place, but the surrounding area was a cesspool of gun stores, pawnshops, and crack houses. While *Adventura by the Sea*, where Valerie resided, looked like a promotional vacation travel brochure come to life. Surrounded by lush green, foliage, a blue sky, inviting water, and pristine white brick buildings with splashes of pastels—it was the perfect enclave for a femme fatale Goddess.

Despite my current status as a struggling piker, I did at least have a decent ride. So I could hold my head high as I pulled up to the apartment complexes security check-in at Valerie's complex.

During my college years, via a connection from one of the Pitt boosters, I was able to land a summer job each year at a place called The Richey Metal Factory, kind of a specialty steel mill that took in scrap metal and melted it into alloys for resale. Working there was like being in burning pits of hell itself for ten hours at a time each shift. The work was back-breaking. It killed my social life because between that and the gym, the only other thing I could do was sleep. And God knows how many toxic chemicals we were breathing in at that hell hole of smoke and fire. But the pay was damn good—thirteen bucks an hour. And with tuition and books taken care of, I was able to save enough by my senior year to buy a new, 1987 5.0 Mustang. It was black and badass. A gear head neighborhood friend tinkered with it, putting a power clutch in and installing something else I don' quite understand that jacked up the horsepower to over 350. So yeah, I lived in a shared apartment surrounded by gun stores, pawnshops, and crack houses. But at least I had a sweet ride.

The guard instructed me where to park my 5.0. Then I gathered myself and headed into the posh lobby, where an actual doorman was there to greet me and direct me to the correct elevator after I gave him Valerie's name.

A few moments later, I knocked on her door. Then when the door opened, I was knocked out all over again by the sheer overwhelming power of her physical presence.

As soon as the door opened, I drank in her dazzling smile and intoxicating smell as she gave me a quick tour of her place.

Blazing whites, rich blacks, with lots of pastel pinks and blueish aquas splashed about in just the right places. All of it brilliantly lit from the hue of the blue sky above the ocean view that dominated outside the floor to ceiling windows of the sliding doors to the balcony. The director in me immediately saw the entire art deco styled sprawling apartment as a perfect movie set.

I wondered for a brief second what she did to be able to afford this paradise perch by the sea. Family money? Then Shelia's warning buzzed in my head about the crowd she ran with. But those thoughts were drowned out and deleted as soon as I turned and gazed back at Valerie. I really didn't care about where her money came from or who she was hanging out with. I just wanted her. And not just in *that* way. Yes, I did want that. Oh, I wanted it bad. Very bad indeed. But it was much more than that. I just wanted to be around her.

Her top was a form-fitting sleeveless vest that hugged the curves of her waist, showcasing her cleavage, mounds of perfectly formed, lightly tanned sculpted flesh. She wasn't huge or super voluptuous. She was just the right size. She was perfect.

She wore a clingy, crayon blue short skirt that hugged the high-arching curves of her ass. Down below those long, lean muscled legs that went on for days, she wore a pair of mustard-colored pumps with a low heel, but still high enough to give her a slight height advantage over me, something that somehow turned me on more than I already was. She was the ultimate alpha female.

And she had the cutest alpha male cat, a thick-bodied, bright-eyed gray tabby named Tommy, who leaped up onto the barstool to check me out before rolling over and demanding a belly rub with his loud purrs.

"You passed the first test," Valerie said. "He likes you."

She came over and petted Tommy while giving me a look that told me that she approved too. I felt like things were off to a promising start.

"Well, shall we?" she said, smiling.

She took my arm, and we headed out to the elevator down to the lobby. I told her to wait there while I trotted out to get the 5.0 and swing it around to pick her up.

I opened the door for her. When I went around to the driver's side and swung down into the seat, I noticed she already turned on the radio. It was set to a local FM pop station, Y-100. The song playing was *You Got it All* by the Jets, a moody piece of soulful sentimental pop that felt more like a song from 1979 that would have played during a lady's choice slow skate at the roller skating rink I hung out during that adolescent summer. Valerie must have liked the tune because she turned up the radio and smiled at me. If this were a movie, it was the exact song I would have chosen for the scene.

"So where to?" I asked.

"South Beach," she said.

"Oh? Really?" I asked.

"You ever hear of Joe's Stone Crab?" she said.

"Oh yeah. Shelia ordered some to go for a birthday party she had, and I went and picked it up for her," I said.

"And? You like?" she asked.

"You kidding me? It was awesome," I said. "But I heard getting a table to dine in there, is pretty much impossible."

"Well there, Rem Rasso, my soon to be director," she said. "I specialize in the impossible."

"Oh? Is that a fact?" I asked.

"It is," she said.

"What, are you like a celebrity or something?" I asked.

She looked over at me and teasingly smiled.

"Or something," she said.

I shifted from fourth to fifth gear as we merged onto I-95 South and rested my hand on the shifter as I usually did. She put her hand on top of mine, and ever so gently caressed the top of my fingertips. It was the most pleasurable touch I had ever felt. Ten minutes into this date with a Goddess, and I was already smitten.

Chapter 4 – South Beach

South Beach was insane.

Sitting in the bumper to bumper traffic on Collins Avenue felt like being in the middle of spring break, but for adults and celebrities. Or at least a lot of people that wanted to look and act like celebrities.

Valerie knew exactly where to turn off and park. It was a vacant lot up a back alley where the cars were packed in like sardines. The entrance was manned by a juiced-up giant that looked like Brutus from *Popeye*. When a pimply-faced kid in a valet uniform sprinted up to me, I was hesitant to turn my ride over to him. The thought of him cramming my 5.0 into that packed lot made me cringe with uneasy terror.

Valerie could see my hesitation to get out of the car.

"It's okay," she said. "You can trust these people. They won't fuck your car up. Trust me."

I nodded and took her word for it. I would have probably taken her word on anything at this point.

So I stepped out of the car and turned it over to the pimply-faced valet before walking over and handing Brutus a twenty to cover the parking fee. He grunted, and I took that to mean I'd better tip this bastard or risk him looking the other way when the local gang of car thieves came lurking around. So I handed him another twenty. He smiled, nodded, and now I felt much better about leaving my ride here.

Perhaps growing impatient about my obsessing over the only asset to my name, Valerie took me by the hand and set a brisk walking pace as we went up the alley and turned right onto the teeming sidewalk of Collins Avenue.

It felt really good holding her hand, and I think it felt good for her too because a few times during our walk, she pulled herself in closer to me, smiled and brushed her cheek across mine. The touch of her skin combined with the lightness her addictive scent was having a euphoric effect on me, an effect that was enhanced further by the sensory overload of the lights, people, combined with the ambiance of music, traffic, and the patio sidewalk festivities that seemed endless.

After a few blocks, we arrived at Joe's Stone Crab, and true to reputation, there was a line to get in the place that snaked around the block. But Valerie walked us right past (and in front of) all of them, earning us a few profane shout-outs from the line of famished would-be patrons.

As soon as we approached the front door, a big, slick-looking Italian guy is a white Don Johnson *Miami Vice* jacket was there to greet us.

I recognized him. It was the Guido who had picked her up in the BMW at Sheila's house that day. He nodded to Valerie.

"You're all set, Val," he said.

He offered me a strong handshake and a friendly smile.

"Tony," he said.

"Rem," I answered.

"Nice to meet you, dude," he said. "Follow me. I got you a booth. Nice and private."

We followed Tony, and it was indeed a sweet spot, up on a raised area, offering a view of the place but far away from the crazy loud, large party tables.

Being not quite sure what was appropriate, I pulled out I twenty for Tony, but he waved it off.

"Val here's got you all taken care of," he said. "And I can't wait to see her in your movie."

It took me a second to wrap my brain around the last part. Because it was simultaneously both awesome and terrifying. The fact that she was excited enough about being asked to be in this movie that she told someone was a good thing. But that also meant she probably thought things were much further along than they actually were.

I had better find financing, find some fast, or risk losing her interest—in the film and in me.

"She's going to light it up," was my response to Tony. "She'll be amazing."

"No doubt," Tony said. "Enjoy your dinner, guys."

As Tony left and we got situated, Valerie gave me a look. A warm, inviting look. A look that made me melt.

Her, the place, the food, the feel-good atmosphere.

The first act of this date was off to the best start imaginable. I could not have scripted it any better myself.

Then, at the end of dinner, while having a drink, Valerie took it up to another level with a surprise under the table. She slipped out of the mustard pumps and slowly moved her exquisite barefoot up along my shin, down across the inside of my thigh, rubbing the ball of her arched foot and perfectly pedicured pink toes up into my groin.

She shot me a devious smile as if knowing it was going to take all the concentration I could muster to calm down enough to walk out of there without embarrassment. But mercifully, she relented her torturous tease, and soon we left. Once again, I was unable to pay a dime as Tony came over to reiterate it was all taken care of.

We left the restaurant and stepped back out into the teeming mass of colorful characters swarming up and down Collins Avenue. Valerie took my hand again, this time holding me close as we walked.

"Well, since this is your agenda tonight, an agenda I am liking very much by the way, where to next?" I asked.

"Some music," she said. "Live music. You like jazz?"

"I do indeed," I said.

"Okay, that's something of an automatic response that any dude will say on a date, especially when he's looking to get laid," she said. "So I'm going to call you on it. Name names. Who in jazz, do you like?"

"Whoa. Let's not just skip over that other part you said," I said.

"Oh, you heard that part, huh? Got your attention, did it?" she said.

"Ummm…yeah. You bet it did," I said.

"Well, all of that might just depend on how you answer the question. Because I'm not about to start fucking some guy who's full of shit," she said. "So come on, Rem Rasso. Name names there, Mister Jazz man."

I looked over at her and returned her teasing smile with one of my own.

"You have no idea who you're dealing with here, do you?" I said.

"Come on," she said. "Stop stalling."

I paused to milk the suspense a bit. Then I let it rip.

"Well, let's start with my favorite in modern Jazz, or what some would term Jazz Fusion or even Pop Jazz, probably the kind of band you'd find playing at a club around here," I said. "My favorites include David Sanborn—whom I absolutely love, Najee—also love, because yeah, I'm a sax guy. But I'm also a trumpet guy, hence Chuck Mangione, because it *Feels So Damn Good.* Then there's Chick Corea, and of course the namesake of the band from which he spawned, the legendary Miles Davis and his antecedent, the also legendary Johnny Coltrane, and of course, all of their antecedents, and perhaps the greatest American composer of all time, Duke Ellington."

I paused for dramatic effect then went into a speeded-up crescendo.

"Back to modern Jazz. The Yellow Jackets—really dug their tunes on the *Star Trek IV: The Voyage Home* soundtrack, where they worked in conjunction with another legend, the avant-garde film composer Leonard Rosenman. Another great film composer, David Grusin, is also an awesome keyboard player and has put out too many great jazz albums to name here. Also related to film, I like Tom Scott and the LA Express, Stanley Clarke, Herbie Hancock, John Barry—remember, he got his start doing Big Band slash jazz, as did John Williams a.k.a. Johnny Williams with those big band swing style comedy scores he did in the sixties. In the non-film category, I also like Pat Methany and…"

"Okay, okay," she interrupted. "Now you're just showing off. So you're not full of shit, I guess."

"Well, that is up for debate," I said. "But, I do know my movies and my music."

She swung in close to me. Her face right up against me.

Her eyes locked onto mine. I could smell the wine from dinner. Combined with her own natural sweet breath, it was drawing me in. But I resisted kissing her right here out in the open on the street, for fear that once I started, I would not be able to stop. So instead, I uttered the cheesiest line imaginable.

"And I know what I like," I said.

If it was a line of dialogue in a movie, I would have ripped on it. But somehow, in this real-time moment between Valerie and me, as on the nose and over the top as it was, it just felt right.

We spent the next hour or so in a club called The Blue Café, and there was indeed live Jazz music featuring a David Sanborn/Najee type saxophone player in a five-piece band with a sultry female vocalist. They were damn good, and as the night went on, I could feel the attraction between Valerie and me intensifying and solidifying into something that felt solid and real. Something beyond the lust. But the lust was there, and she was as anxious as I was to close out of our bar tab and head out. And this time, I actually got to pay.

Then, walking back to the car, hand in hand, in the midst of euphoric bliss, each of us eagerly anticipating what was going to happen soon, we walked smack dab into the middle of a shrieking buzzkill.

It was a jacked-up pick-up truck sporting cartoon giant wheels with a Confederate flag sticking out of the top of the cab right next to the gun rack.

The truck pulled up to the intersection we were crossing, gunning the engine, intentionally spewing black exhaust in our direction.

I knew this was going to be trouble even before these yahoos began hooting and hollering, revealing themselves to be the assholes they were. The driver and the passenger were loudmouth punks. The two in the back cab were decent sized, mean-looking, tattooed skinheads. At least one of the tattoos was a swastika.

Yeah, I knew this was going to be trouble. Because I know me.

I'm an easy-going guy. Intense in the classic "type A" you would expect any obsessive artist to be. But certainly not violent. A lover, not a fighter.

But I do have this one thing. This flaw. A temper. It doesn't blow often. It takes a lot. But when it goes. It's not pretty. It's downright scary. It certainly scares me. And as soon as these bullying inbred assholes descended upon us in there bullying, designed to intimidate Confederate flag wearing monster truck, I could feel the red alert klaxon sounding off inside me.

Yeah, this was going to be trouble.

So when the punk in the passenger's side directed his harassing vulgar venom at Valerie, I reacted.

I sprung forward, placing my coiled form between the truck and Valerie, and glared right at the gap-toothed cackling greasy-haired asshole hanging out the passenger side who had led the demeaning chants toward Valerie.

He gave me a mocking look and then directed a leering glare at Valerie.

"Hey, pretty boy," he cackled. "Howz about you get your faggy disco ass out of here so we can take your girlfriend there for a little ride and show her a few things."

I saw red, my rage thermometer cascading into the stratosphere.

"Hey! Fuck you! You little cunt," I screamed with a thundering force, making sure he, everyone in the truck, and the entire city block, heard me loud and clear.

For a second, there was no response from any of the occupants of the monster truck, as if they were in shock over the fact that anyone, especially some young not all that scary looking guy who was alone with a date—would dare to challenge them.

But challenge them I did. They knew it, and every single person and car at this jam-packed intersection knew it as well.

"What did you say to me?" Gap Tooth squawked, trying to get his tough guy persona going to save face in front of his boys.

"You heard me, asshole," I said. "Or are you deaf, in addition to being a retarded inbred white supremacist piece of shit?"

There was another beat of silence with no reaction. That shock factor again.

He was sizing me up, and even though I did not look mean or scary and was a lot smaller than my college linebacker days, I still had some muscle size, looked athletic, and Gap Tooth wanted no part of me.

At least not in a fair fight.

The driver yelled something into the back cab—some kind of order to the two skinhead goons back there. Then, both of these enforcers leaped down from the cab, each taking a side next to Gap Tooth's still closed passenger door.

Flanked by these goons, Gap Tooth now felt comfortable enough to step out of the monster truck. No, not just comfortable. Now, he was downright cocky having these two formidable thugs as bookends, both of whom had four of five inches on me in height and about thirty pounds in weight.

Gap Tooth started sneering and cackling some more, then made an obscene gesture with his tongue at Valerie.

"Oh, you were saying?" Gap Tooth hissed.

"I was saying that if you do that again, I'll break your fucking jaw," I said as a matter-of-factly.

"Oh? You mean this?" Gap Tooth said.

He made the obscene gesture with his tongue at Valerie again.

Then he sneered and cackled some more.

The two skinhead goons joined in on the mocking laughter.

I let the laughter die down. Feeling secure now that he was flanked by his two enforcers, Gap Tooth took a step closer and attempted to stare me down as if I was to be intimidated.

I broke the tense silence.

"Because I'm a nice guy and because I'm really not looking to hurt anyone here tonight, I'm going to give you one more chance to stay out of the hospital," I said, as calmly and as firmly as such a line could be delivered in real life, especially as my psychotic hair-trigger temper began to boil over inside me.

"Apologize to the lady," I demanded. "Now!"

Gap Tooth looked over at his two skinhead goons as if to say, "Can you believe this guy?"

Then, all three laughed again, but louder, and with even more poisonous, mocking disdain. I could feel myself being sprayed by Gap Tooth's foul breath and his toxic saliva.

I saw red again, but worse.

I did not think. I just reacted.

With every coiled-up ounce of core strength that I possessed, I rotated my torso, drove with the full force of my legs and hip, blasting Gap Tooth with a left hook.

The punch landed with a cracking thud that echoed up and down Collins Avenue.

I have no idea whether I made good on my promise to break his jaw, but I was pretty sure he would be concussed. The punch lifted him off the ground, and I watched his hideous little pinhead snap back. Then, he collapsed, going down to the ground like a wet noodle.

But I knew the battle was not over. I had these two racist thugs to deal with, and I knew by their size and demeanor, they would not go down so easy, and it was two on one.

I wasted no time.

I snapped back to the left and drove my knee into the first goon's balls before splattering his nose with a vicious head butt. Then I went after the other skinhead with everything I had.

I went completely savage, letting my demonic temper take over in a way that must have scared the hell out of the crowd. I was relentless, driving him into the ground, beating him to a pulp—until I looked up and saw the barrel of a long rifle pointed straight at me.

In all the commotion, I had lost track of the driver. And now, he was about to end my life. I was sure of it.

Then, just as I could see his finger about to squeeze down on the trigger, my would-be murderer toppled to the ground, and the rifle fell to the pavement.

Standing behind his fallen form, holding the butt of a pistol, was the man who was my savior.

He was black and just seemed to ooze coolness as if dealing with characters like these assholes was something he did on a regular basis.

Dressed sharply, but in a conservative gray suit, he wore round wire-rim glasses. He looked more Wall Street than gangster. And he was so damn calm. Calm as a freaking cucumber. Like he had ice in his veins.

He was flanked by two enforcers that looked like extras from a *Miami Vice* episode. They were either Italian or Latin, and huge. The bulging holsters underneath their silk suit jackets indicated they were armed as well. One of them had scooped up the long gun from the pavement.

My rescuer pointed his pistol at the monster truck driver and Gap Tooth, who were both staggering to their feet.

"Collect your filthy trash," he said, motioning down to the two skinheads I had taken out, who were not recovering quite as fast.

"And get the fuck out here," he said. "Now!"

The four racist and now bloodied-up punks obeyed, climbing up into their Confederate monster truck, puttering away into the now beginning to move traffic of Collins Avenue.

Valerie was now at my side. She hugged me and held my hand. Then she looked at me in a way that stirred me inside. It was a look of deep appreciation, mixed with intense lust and even love. Yes, love. Maybe it was the heightened drama of the moment. Maybe it was my imagination. But I could sense that Valerie felt something for me. Something that was building between us and escalating at an alarming rate.

Then, as my rescuer approached and introduced himself to me as Charlie, I saw him and Valerie exchange looks and nods.

Valerie knew Charlie.

I felt like I was about to find out more, but before we could engage in a conversation, Miami's finest came rushing onto the scene via the flashing lights of two squad cars. Took them long enough, I thought. But in reality, everything probably happened within three minutes. Real-life fights rarely last more than thirty seconds because people either get hurt or stop from exhaustion.

The cop cars did not even phase Charlie. He just looked back at them as if this was a business matter he had to attend to. Which, I was guessing, was exactly what it was.

"I'll take care of this," Charlie said, nodding back at the flashing lights.

"You two go on and enjoy the rest of your evening," he added before turning and walking away.

Valerie took my hand, leading me away from the crowded street.

"What now?" I asked as we headed back up the alley where my car was parked.

"We are going to do exactly what he said," Valerie replied. "Enjoy the rest of our night—to the absolute fullest."

She looked at me, teasingly. Lovingly. Lustfully. Even sinfully.

Driving back up to Adventura, all of a sudden, the dramatic showdown and fisticuffs seemed like they had happened hours, if not days ago. My mind, every frame of my mental and emotional focus, was zeroed in on only one thing.

Valerie, and how I wanted her. More desperately than I ever wanted anything in my life before.

The clothes could not have come off any faster.

We stepped into Valerie's apartment, and it was as if we both were naked in an instant, our bodies molding and melding together, groping, stroking, probing, holding each other in utter desperation, as if we were both in primal heat.

The tonguing and the thrusting started right there, up against the wall and down onto the entrance mat by the front door, before continuing with even more white-hot intensity in her bedroom, on top of the luxurious white spread.

It was like living inside an Adrian Lyne film, the director of *9 ½ weeks*. I was the young naïve seeker, the obsessive voyeur. And she, the embodiment of a high-end, classy Miami society woman unleashing the wild slut within her. All of it filmed in glorious wide-screen Panavision.

As the burning intensity of our physicality propelled us to ascending layers of insane spastic pleasure toward the inevitable explosive climax, all I could think about was that her touch and taste was every bit as exquisite as her look and smell. She was, in every way I could imagine, hope, or lust for, complete and utter perfection. Like a character straight out of an erotic thriller. A real-life femme fatale Goddess.

Hours later, when daylight announced itself with sparkling hues of golden light reflected from the glassy water from beyond the balcony doors of the bedroom, I wished I had a camera, preferably a Super 16mm Aaton handheld, to capture the scene. It was the stuff of a cinematographer's wet dream.

While Valerie continued to sleep—her impossibly long, shapely limbs lit by the golden morning light as they peeked out from the covers—I headed out into the kitchen and found my way around enough to put on a pot of coffee.

I scanned through the fridge and cupboards looking for something to eat and came upon a box of Bisquick pancake batter, some fresh blueberries, and maple syrup. Jackpot, I thought.

Waking up to a breakfast of fresh coffee and pancakes would make Valerie happy, and right now, all I wanted was to please her. A romantic would say I was smitten and falling in love. A cynical macho man would call me pussy-whipped. I suppose they would both be right.

As I was mixing up the pancake batter, there was a sudden knock at the door.

My heart skipped a nervous beat, wondering just who in the fuck that could be at this hour in the morning.

I opened the door and was greeted by Charlie, my ice in his veins, well-dressed rescuer from last night. He was clad in another suit, more casual and slick than the one from last night—a tan Armani. Both his appearance and demeanor were every bit as meticulous and measured as I remembered.

And once again, he was flanked by two Latin/Italian looking bodyguards. Not as big as the guys from last night, but they looked every bit as formidable.

"May I?" he asked, motioning to come in.

He could see my hesitation.

"Not my place to say really," I said. "Because it's not my place."

"I can assure you, Mr. Rasso, Valerie would be okay with it. More than okay," Charlie said.

"Oh?" I asked, already having guessed from last night that they knew each other.

"We are associates who work for the same employer," he said.

I nodded, stood aside, and opened the door for them.

Once the three of them were inside, Charlie pivoted to face me.

"And that mutual employer is interested in you, Mr. Rasso," he said.

For a second, I had to remind myself this was real because the whole scene, especially coming off the heels of last night, was so freaking bizarre. I suddenly remembered my cousin Sheila's warning about the characters that Valerie ran with.

"Charlie, first, thanks again for saving my ass last night. Really," I said. "And second, it's was too early in the morning to be so…so informal. So please, it's Rem."

He nodded affirmatively.

"And third, why does your boss want to see me?" I said.

"Let's just say, he's interested in your handiwork," Charlie said.

"What? You mean the fight?" I asked.

I looked at each of the bodyguards, then back to Charlie.

"Looks to me like you already are all good to go in the muscle department," I said.

Then, I turned to see Valerie standing by the kitchen in a bathrobe. She locked her gaze onto Charlie, and she did not look pleased.

"Charlie, you leave him out of this," she said. "You know the rules. My deal does not extend to my friends."

"Oh? Just a friend?" Charlie said, seeming to want to irritate her.

"Or, to who am I fucking," she said. "So take your two Gumbas here, and fuck off."

For the first time, Charlie looked a bit rattled. Thrown off his delivery.

"Look, Val. It's not like that," Charlie said. "He just wants to meet the man. You know how Jerry is with his college football."

Charlie turned to look at me.

"And Rem here is a two-time All American," Charlie said, turning toward me. "Ain't that right?"

I nodded in the affirmative, trying not to look like I was feigning modesty. Truth be told, that part of my life was over and felt like a lifetime ago. All that mattered now was getting my movie made. But still, I admit, it always feels good to get recognition for something you accomplished.

"Saw you live and in-person myself when you came down here to the Orange Bowl last year and kept Pitt competitive in a game they had no business being in. Against what might have been the greatest talent of college football ever assembled on one team."

If he was trying to butter me up, he knew exactly what buttons to push. My anxiety dissipated, and now I was actually intrigued to meet this Jerry.

"Actually, I'm going to have to disagree with you on that one and go with the Pitt team of 1981," I said. "Not that I'm biased or anything."

"Well…a case could be made, I'll give you that," Charlie said. "But if you're going go with a Pitt team, you go with 1980 because of the defense. I mean Hugh Green and Ricky Jackson."

"Touché," I said.

"So, All American linebacker and part-time Mike Tyson impersonator Rem Rasso. Jerry would like you over to his house for lunch at one," Charlie said.

"Valerie knows the way," Charlie added, turning toward her. "And, of course, is invited too."

"No thanks," Valerie said, looking even more irritated. "Saturday's our biggest day at the shop. Tell Jerry I have a business to run. I'm sure he'll understand."

With that, she turned and made a firm exit, disappearing back down the hallway toward the bedroom, her long body gently swaying under the robe. Her bare, silky, perfect feet gliding along the custom-made burnt orange tile floor.

Watching her walk was hypnotic and reminded me of exactly what had attracted me to her off the charts seductive presence in the first place. Namely, getting her on film.

I needed to get this movie made. And even though I knew Valerie was dead said against me meeting this enigmatic Jerry—and probably with good reason—maybe this was an opportunity to help get my movie made. This guy might be dangerous. He might be a gangster. Or he might just be an asshole. But I was certain of one thing. He must have money.

Rule one of Independent Filmmaking is write a good script.

Rule two is cast a strong lead.

Rule three, get investors. Movies don't get made without money.

So despite Valerie's implied warning and my own Spidey sense tingling, I plunged ahead.

"Okay, Charlie," I said. "Tell your boss, I'll be there."

Chapter 6 – Jerry's Lair

He was known as King of the Grove, a.k.a, King Jerry.

Valerie gave me the backstory on Jerry as I drove her to Adventura Mall to open her fashion shop/clothing store, a trendy retail hot spot dubbed *Miami Styles*.

I remembered seeing a write-up on the store in the Miami Herald. It was the hip place to shop in the city. I began to wonder just what this Jerry character had to do with the shop or Valerie for that matter. Was "the deal" she spoke of this morning about Jerry owning a piece of the shop? It was the only thing that made sense.

Jerry Strombolo was a fifty-something-year-old Captain in the Colombo crime family. He rubbed so many people the wrong way in New York that they sent him down here to run the Miami operation just to "get the fat fuck out of town," according to Valerie.

"So he's an asshole, and they banished him?" I said.

"Sort of. But that doesn't make him any less powerful," she said. "All they care about in New York is how much money he is making for them, and thanks, to Charlie—who actually runs the business—they are making a fortune."

"So Charlie makes everybody back home fat, and Jerry gets all the credit."

"Something like that," Valerie said. "But I'm sure they have some idea what's going on. They have to know Jerry is too ignorant and too lazy to be responsible. And make no mistake, Charlie is very smart and very shrewd about covering his ass. But they need Jerry down here anyway. The whole made man, full-blooded Italian bullshit."

"So, what's the deal with Jerry and you?" I asked point-blank.

She punted, and I thought it was best not to press the issue. But I could tell she was nervous. Nervous for me, I was guessing, and I had never seen her nervous before. Was he muscling her? Squeezing her business for profits? I wondered just what the hell I was getting into.

Valeria was too concerned about my meeting with this South Florida Kingpin to stay at work, so she had me hang out at the mall for a bit, then accompanied me on the drive down into the heart of Coconut Grove where Jerry resided, in a gaudy mansion that screamed 1980s Miami. It was an opulent art deco palace of obscene excess that looked like a replica of Al Pacino's house in *Scarface.*

A trio of armed guards in suits opened a cast-iron gate that led up into a long, circular, red brick driveway. As we drove up to the house entrance, Valerie squeezed my hand, looked at me, and issued a warning.

"He is very manipulative, can be very intimidating, but also very charming," she said. "Just be careful."

She kissed me on the lips before we exited the car, then we walked past two more armed guards before a butler or doorman of some kind opened up a pair of gold plated doors and directed us inside to a sprawling dining room with marble floors and a vaulted ceiling that was ridiculously high.

There were mounted TVs along all of the walls, each playing a different sporting event of some kind. I assumed that gambling was a large part of the family business. It seemed that everything that was movie gangster cliché was actually true when it came to real-life gangsters.

Then, a door swung open from the opposite direction that we had come in, and there he was. Making a dramatic entrance that looked like something I might have blocked out in a scene I was directing.

Flanked by yet two more bodyguards, plus Charlie right behind them.

Jerry walked toward us, then his three-hundred plus form stopped with a lumbering thud. He stood about six feet away and glared at me.

"You know, if you want to keep dating my girl Valerie here, you're going to have to get my blessing first there, tough guy," Jerry said.

There was an eternal—and very uncomfortable—moment of tense silence.

Then Jerry busted out into over-the-top laughter, as did the bodyguards and Charlie.

"Oh, I'm just fucking with you, kid," Jerry said. "Valerie does whatever the hell she wants anyway. So I have learned."

It seemed to be a dig at Valerie, and it definitely annoyed her.

"Besides, I have heard nothing but great things about you," Jerry said.

"About last night from Charlie. And remind me not to piss you off. I heard all about that left hook there, Mr. Balboa," he said.

"And I heard good things about you from your boss, the manager at the gym where you work," he added. "Says you're a real hard worker. Reliable and a good guy."

I was completely caught off guard.

"But…how?"

"Hard Bodies Gym. I own the fucking joint. Well, unofficially, of course. I provided the seed money for that place," he said boastfully. "You know, these damn banks, so hard for the small guy to get a loan these days. So, they come to King Jerry. Hell, I own eighty percent of the businesses in Coral Gables."

"And in Adventura too," he added while looking at Val.

"But I'm sure Val told you all about how it was me that gave her the big break," he said. "When nobody else would give her the time of day. Ain't that right, Val?"

Valerie just glared. Jerry looked smarmy and satisfied.

Manipulative, bullying, controlling…yeah, I was beginning to get the picture.

I did not say anything. I just held my breath, waiting for the unbearable tension to die down. Thank god a lady Chef and her assistant swung open the doors, wheeling in several platters of food and drink.

"Ahh, lunch is served," Jerry said.

I wondered just how the hell I would be able to eat with my stomach tied up in knots. I had no idea what to expect next from this character Jerry. He seemed so wound up, so on edge. I wondered if he might be on cocaine. Or was a sociopath. Or a psychopath. Or all three.

It was going to be the longest lunch ever.

According to movies and other popular media, there are two major types of gangsters.

The ice-cold killer—a deep, methodical thinker who calmly operates and speaks in a low, but firm voice. Michael Corleone would fall into this category, as would the real-life example sitting here at the lunch table, Charlie. The other type would be the loud, flamboyant, volatile psychopath, always coming across as about explode in a fit of violence. A good example of this would be the infamous real-life Gambino Family Boss, John Gotti.

Jerry Strombolo definitely fell into the latter category. But as the still silently seething Valerie had warned me, he could be very charming. Plus, he did know his football, and it was there that we bonded over lunch without me even realizing it.

He wanted to know all about my Pitt days, especially any of my experiences with Dan Marino.

So I entertained the table with tales of my freshman year on the scout team, where I faced the future NFL record-breaker during the daily grind of essentially getting the shit beat out of me by an offensive line bigger and stronger than most of the pro teams at the time. Jerry, in particular, loved hearing the story about the time I failed to get my head around fast enough when downfield, covering a pass route, and took one of Marino's lasers square in the upper back.

"The force of the ball actually cracked my shoulder pads," I said. "The bruise was nasty. I had trouble breathing for a week."

Then as the lunch wound down, Jerry got to the point—the reason he had summed me to his gaudy gangster lair here in the heart of Coconut Grove.

"So, like I said before, I'm in the money business," Jerry said, lighting up a real Cuban cigar after offering me one which a politely turned down.

"Because banks suck, and make it so hard for the average Joe or Sally to get a decent loan, the demand for my services is off the fucking charts, I shit you not Rem," he said.

"But, there is one problem about being in the money business," Jerry said. "Tell him what it is, Charlie."

"Payments," Charlie said. "Sometimes, Joe or Sally decides they do not want to honor the arrangement we make with them."

"Exactly. And that can be a problem. A big fucking problem," Jerry said. "Which is where you come in, Rem."

"What?" I asked. "Me?"

I glanced over at Valerie. She looked horrified. Her eyes begging me not to fall into his seductive trap.

"Jerry. I really appreciate it," I said as carefully as I could. "But if you're looking for a collector, I'm not your guy. Don't read too much into last night. I am not a tough guy."

Jerry just laughed. It seemed like a good nature laugh. But still, it made me nervous. There was that psychopathic edge to it.

"Not a tough guy?" Jerry said.

He looked at Charlie and repeated himself.

"Not a tough guy?" he said.

"Bullshit!" he added. "You beat the fuck out of three Nazis last night and played linebacker at an elite division one football program at what…two-hundred pounds soaking wet?"

"Well, I was bigger at the time," I said. "About two-twenty five."

"Yeah? Maybe you weighed that going to camp after an offseason of living in the weight room and eating six times a day, but you played at two-hundred," Jerry said. "Hey, I know my shit. I fucking make a living gambling on football."

The fucker did know his football. I reluctantly nodded, hoping he knew it did not mean I was saying yes to the job.

"But I don't get it," I said. "You are packed to the rafters with guys around here twice my size that look like legitimate tough guys, which again, I am not. Why would you need me, anyway?"

"Because all those guys are marked in a Fed or Dade County organized crime taskforce file somewhere. Most of them can't take a piss without a cop following them, let alone conduct my business."

"But you…you, my friend, are an unknown. You are my joker. My ace in the hole. My secret weapon," Jerry said.

"That is why I need you," he said.

Then he delivered his closing line and did so with great conviction.

"And I could make it all so worth your while," he said. "You have no idea."

Then, Jerry did what all great salespeople did when they knew it was the right moment. He shut up, smiled, and looked me in the eye.

I had no idea what fuck to do to get out of this.

Then, I looked at the distraught Valerie, and it occurred to me.

"Again, Mr. Strombolo, I am appreciative. For you having us over for this great lunch. And of the offer," I said.

"But I have my own thing going on," I added. "A job…in a sense. Not the gym. Something else. Something real. Something big."

I was sure Jerry was not accustomed to being turned down.

For a second, I could sense he was about to display his volatile psychopathic nature. Have us thrown out. Or worse. Beaten. Shot. Who knows? But then, he seemed to calm down when he looked to Charlie.

"Oh, that's right. The movie thing," he said, adding a dismissive wave of his hand.

"You know about that?" I asked.

"Hey, Remmy, nothing escapes me," he said. "King Jerry knows everything going on around here. This is my town. Don't you ever forget that."

Evidently, Tony, who seemed to serve as Valerie's chauffeur when he wasn't managing a restaurant, was also a gossip.

"But from what I can gather, you don't really have a movie yet. Do you? " Jerry said. "That is… until you have the money to make it."

"True," I said.

Then I went down a path that Valerie had warned me against.

As soon as I opened my mouth, I knew deep down inside, this was all going to a very uncomfortable place. A dangerous place. But I needed to get my movie made, no matter what. Because to truly be a movie director, I needed to make movie. And if I was not a director, what was I?

"Which is why I am currently looking for an investor," I said.

"Someone who wants to take a chance on investing in the next big hit independent film," I added. "Think *Night of the Living Dead*. Think *Halloween*. Think *Friday the 13th*. Think *The Terminator*."

A beat of dead silence passed as Jerry chomped on his cigar. Charlie looked intrigued. Valerie horrified. The Gumba bodyguards, entertained.

"So explain to me about the movie business," Jerry said.

Now it was my turn to sell the salesman.

I explained that there were one-hundred points in a movie and that fifty were used to pay the cast and crew (with the bulk going to the leads and director) and 50 for investors. I told him I needed to raise one-hundred fifty thousand (this was based on my directing professor's estimate after breaking down my script with a production manager). So each point would be a three thousand dollar investment.

"That's all fascinating stuff, kid," Jerry quipped. "But how do I make any money."

"There are several ways," I waxed on. This was a conversation in my sweet spot.

"I enter the movie into the Coconut Grove Film Festival this August—which I will be doing—and it gets some buzz. Either by winning some prizes, getting a good review in the Miami Herald, or just by strong word mouth," I said. "And this attracts the attention of distributors and producers from studios who are there shopping for products to keep their pipelines filled."

I paused for a dramatic effect before ramping into my closing argument.

"The first example is the easiest and most common," I said. "A pick-up deal. A studio just buys the movie outright to do with it as it pleases. The average pickup deal for an indie film of this genre is seven-hundred fifty thousand. So that's three-hundred seventy-five thousand for the investors. A return of one-hundred-fifty percent."

"Now scenario two is more complicated, but unlimited," I went on.

"After the awards, the reviews, and word of mouth, offers start to pour in. A distributor offers to fund a worldwide theatrical release and pick up the tab for a cut in the gross. Let's call it fifty percent to make the math easy. But it will be lower than that. That means for every dollar in ticket sales, the theater gets half, then half goes back to the distributor and the owners of the film—those one-hundred points. Let's say the movie does ten million—a very easy number to hit with any decent distribution and marketing package. After the distributor and theater owners take their cut, that's two point five million to the owners of the film, one point two five million to the investors. That's almost ten times your money. And if the film really hits—in a *Halloween*, *Friday the 13th*, *Terminator* kind of way, the returns would be fucking insane. We are talking tens of millions of dollars. The sky's the limit."

Then, I did exactly what Jerry had done earlier after pitching me. I shut up and looked him in the eye.

The dead silence was excruciating.

I thought I had him. But then, he had to go all gangster on me and remind me of exactly who I was dealing with here.

"That all sounds swell, but what if I get fucked?" he asked.

"What do you mean? There is no fucking involved," I said. "You own a piece of the movie. The movie makes money. You make money. It's all straight forward."

"And if the movie makes no money? If it's a bust, who's gonna give me my money back?" he barked.

What the fuck?

I almost said that out loud. The next part I actually did say out loud, and probably shouldn't have.

"Come on, man," I said. "You can't have your cake and eat it too."

Everyone looked around nervously. As if expecting Jerry to erupt into a volcanic rage over my words. But he answered calmly and with smug satisfaction.

"Oh, but I can! Maybe you can't. Maybe nobody else in this town can. But you better fucking believe I can have my cake and eat it too," he said. "Because I'm King fucking Jerry."

Maybe I had watched too many gangster movies and cop TV shows, because I found myself on verbal autopilot, talking like I was a guest star on an episode of *Starsky and Hutch*. The thing is, quite often, the guest stars on those shows ended up dead.

"Because you can put that same money out in the street," I said. "Get a hefty weekly vig, and have the principle guaranteed. Well, not really guaranteed. There is that matter of successfully collecting those funds."

"I always collect," Jerry snapped back. "Dead or alive. I always collect."

Even that ominous statement did not make me break character.

"If collecting was that easy, you wouldn't have summoned me here today," I said. "Am I right? So why not make a legitimate investment in something that—although has no guarantees—has a real good chance of making you a lot of money with unlimited upside."

Jerry was red-faced. I thought he was about to blow. Maybe have one his goons shoot me right there on the spot. But instead, he laughed and shook his head as if in disbelief.

"You got some big fucking brass balls, kid. I'll give you that," he said.

As cool and methodical as ever, Charlie stepped forward, looking toward Jerry for permission to take the lead. Jerry gave him a nod yes.

"Rem, bottom line, it just doesn't make business sense for Jerry to throw money at some independent movie with a first time director and no stars," Charlie said. "No offense to you, or to Valerie. You may be the next Alfred fucking Hitchcock and her the second coming of Grace Kelly, and we could still lose our ass on this. Even under the best of circumstances, movies are a notorious risky bet."

He paused for a moment to allow the strength of his argument to sink in before adding, "Am I right?"

His logic was flawless, forcing me to nod in the affirmative.

But I still could not leave well enough alone. Because I still needed money to get my movie made, and the clock was ticking for that looming August Coconut Grove Film Festival.

"I get it," I said. "But what about just a regular loan?"

There was a bit of silence pierced by a shriek from Valerie.

"Rem! No!" she pleaded. "Absolutely not. He will fucking own you."

"No, he won't," I said. "Because we are all going to be clear on the terms. Right?"

I looked at Charlie. Charlie looked to Jerry. Jerry sat back on his chair, took a puff of his Cuban cigar, and nodded yes.

"You sure about this?" Charlie said. "This ain't fucking Barnett Bank. You miss a payment, any payment, and the consequences will be dire."

"I understand," I said.

"On one-hundred fifty thousand principal, those payments will be three thousand dollars a week. Delivery must be made on the seventh day after you receive the principal. You can come right here to the house and give the payment to me personally," Charlie said. "Don't make us come looking for you."

"What about the principle?" I asked.

"Twenty weeks," Jerry chimed in. "Make it September 1st."

"I need more time," I said. "The festival's the first week of August. I need time to work the…"

"September 1st," Jerry said again, but louder. "Or you can go down to the local bank and see how eager they are to foot the bill for your little project."

That was it. The terms were clear enough. And, at least in my mind, if I wanted to get my movie made, I had no other choice.

"Just one thing, so we are absolutely crystal clear," I said. "Once I pay back that principal, we are done. Finito. I owe you nothing. Our business will be concluded. Period."

"You pay me back in full, and that's it," Jerry said. "You go on with your life making movies. And nobody ever needs to know we ever did business."

"Make all your payments on time. Pay us back the one fifty K by September one," Charlie said. "Then, our business is concluded."

I took a deep breath. I looked over at Valerie.

She looked more worried than pissed, but I was going to have to do a little damage control after this to reassure her that I had it all worked out. At least in theory. Twenty weeks of payments was sixty grand. That left ninety grand to actually make the movie. It would be tight as a mother fucker. The bulk of that would have to go to renting cameras, a Steadicam, dollies and track, lighting equipment, and film processing. But I could make it work.

With the full one-hundred points to work with, I could save money by paying in points. Have Val's shop do the wardrobe. I'd give her half of whatever points were left over after I used what I had to for a crew. Have Bobby Z handle the cameras and Steadicam and pay him what he would be making at the gym plus points. Get Shelia's help on production design and shooting locations. And milk help from the film school as much as possible. Get extras and secondary casting from the theater department.

Yes. I could make this work because I *had* to make this work.

"Okay," I said, looking to Charlie, then to Jerry.

"Let's do it."

I found out that Valerie's initial experience with Jerry was eerily similar to mine.

"You don't understand," I pleaded, trying to explain why I did what I did, taking that money, knowing full well the dangerous game I was playing.

"Ever since I first held a Super 8 movie camera in my hand at twelve years old, I knew exactly what I needed to do. Who I needed to become," I said. "George Lucas once said if you haven't accomplished anything by the age of thirty, then chances are you never would. I feel like this is my only shot. I have to do this here and now, no matter what the cost. I have to make this happen, Val. I just have to."

"To quote Michael Nouri from *Flashdance*," I added. "Don't you get it? When you give up your dreams, you die."

She nodded. Manage a smile. Then moved closer to me. I could feel her finally relaxing. Then she opened up to me.

"Oh, I get it," she said. "Believe me, I do."

"I needed money to get the shop started, and just like you, had no other options," she continued.

"And it was all good at first. I never missed a payment. The shop was a huge hit from the start. My designs took off, and within a few months, I had more than enough to pay back the loan."

We were driving into downtown Coconut Grove. I needed to talk to the AMC Theater manager and the property manager of the plaza about securing some shooting time, hopefully for a full mid-morning on a weekday when it would be slow. The film school could secure me the local permits. But I needed the cooperation of these two managers to seal the deal. I had tried approaching them before, and both were…difficult. I was hoping they would respond to a pitch from a different salesperson—Valerie.

"So, what then? You paid the loan back?" I asked.

"No. That's the thing. Jerry wouldn't let me. He insisted that I keep the money and that we were now full partners, him being the silent partner."

"So he pulled a Darth Vadar ala *Empire* and altered the deal," I said.

"Huh? Oh, *The Empire Strikes Back*. The thing with Bill Dee. Yes. Exactly,' she said

"You went along with that?" I asked.

"No! I fought him tooth and nail. But he insisted," Valerie said. "And threatened the business—and me. His exact words were, *well, you know that without my protection, something might happen to your shop. Somebody might even burn it to the ground. With you in it.*"

"Damn," I sighed. "Now, I'm getting the picture."

"It gets worse," she said. "He starts using the business as his personal piggy bank. Kept sending all of his gangster friends' bitch cunt wives and girlfriends over, expecting me to cater to them and give them free shit. That fat fuck became our biggest liability. It became a nightmare."

She went on.

"Another year goes by, the shop gets featured in Style magazine and in Cosmopolitan. I hire more designers and salespeople. We start a mail-order business. Now things are really taking off. So I offer to buy Jerry out at more than fifty percent of the business, just to get him out of my hair. At this point, he is making five times his initial loan. But again, he tells me to fuck off."

She paused a second to gather herself. I could tell this next part was painful for her and at the crux of why she looked at Jerry the way she did, with such bitter, hidden rage.

"So at the time, I had a designer named Robby, and he and I…we were…very close. Not a couple or anything—he was gay—but he was…my best friend. We built the business together…"

Her voice trailed off as emotion overtook her. I nabbed a parking spot, parallel parked the car, reached over and took her hand.

"And Robby…he just wanted to stick up for me, and he was as tired of Jerry's shit as I was. So he went to try and talk to him, offering even more money just to go away."

She stopped and stared off into space for a long moment before finishing.

"I never saw him again."

I just stayed silent for a moment and held her hand. But I knew I had to say something to reassure her—and me—that I did not end up suffering the same fate as Robby.

"Val, listen to me. I wrote *The Return of Amanda* when I was thirteen years-old, and in one way or another, I've been planning out how to turn it into a movie every day since," I said. "I've got my script. I've got the absolute perfect lead. Now, I got my funding. And in a minute, we are going to go in there and nail down our locations."

I looked her in the eyes.

"Trust me. This is going to work. This movie will sell, and we will get a deal," I said.

"But Jerry…you cannot trust him," she said.

"Oh, believe me, I don't," I said. "But what happened to you…you were blindsided. This time, we'll be ready for him. All we need to do is make this movie work. This is our ticket to get that fat fuck out of your life, and to go on and do whatever great adventure we want to move on to next."

She took it all in. Then she smiled and nodded in affirmation.

"We got this," I added.

I could see her transform before me. She now looked not only reassured, but self-confident as usual, focused, and maybe even inspired.

"Okay," she said. "Let's go do this."

With that, we got out of the car, and as I watched Valerie walk up the Coconut Grove Plaza staircase toward the front of the AMC, I was once again mesmerized by her hypnotic walk, her raw physicality, and her supreme confidence. These uptight, repressed property managers had no chance against her magnetic superpowers.

By the end of the morning, our shooting at the Coconut Grove locations would be secured. Meanwhile, Sheila had promised me the Key Biscayne apartment of a snowbird friend of hers to use as the main character Jimmy's place of residence.

Things were coming together, and I refused to let worries about Jerry trying to fuck us, or anything else get in the way. It was all about the movie, and this movie was going to happen.

Now I just needed to fill out the rest of the cast and assemble my crew.

It was time to become a director. A real director.

Guy Meade, my directing professor, was ecstatic at the news that I now had financing, had secured locations, a luminous female lead born to play Amanda, and that I was ready to go into production as soon as I had my team assembled.

"So besides your female lead, what else you got so far," he asked.

"I can get my roommate to handle the Steadicam and be my camera operator," I said. "Guys from the gym as gaffers. My cousin Sheila—she's the one I told you about who was in couple episodes of *Miami Vice*—she's an art director more so than an actress, so she can be my production designer. Valerie, our lead, is a fashion designer who owns Miami Styles up in Adventura, so we're all set for wardrobe."

"Damn, you're like a real Roger Corman there," he said. "You'll be saving a ton of money doing things that way."

"More I can put on the screen," I said. "More for cameras, film stocks, lighting equipment, and a composer."

And more to pay that mother fucking vig to Jerry.

When I wasn't mentally rehearsing my shot list and planning out camera placements, I was running the numbers in my head.

Nineteen weeks till the Festival. Rounding that up to twenty, that meant putting aside sixty grand of the loan to pay the juice. Again, that meant making the movie for ninety grand, paying most of the cast and crew with points, and getting a sweet deal at the festival in order to pay back the principal of the loan—or end up wearing cement shoes at the bottom of the Atlantic Ocean.

"That's a start, but who else do you have? Any production manager?" Professor Meade asked. "Because trust me, the production manager is who makes movies work. They run the set so you can focus on what's in the frame in front of the camera."

"Sharon from class is already is on board as my producer, but yeah, I do need a production manager," I said. "And help with the secondary casting and extras. I have lots of moving Steadicam shots outside in Coconut Grove—a lot of background to fill with people who look real."

"I can help you with all that," he said, opening up his address book as we sat in his office.

"By the way," he said while dialing the phone. "I finally got a chance to read *The Return of Amanda*."

"And?" I asked as his phone dialed on speaker.

"It's the real deal, Rem," he said. "It works. It's a fun read, but remember, it's not a novel. It's a blueprint for movie. Now you have to go out and build it. One shot at a time. One scene at a time. Don't fuck this up, and you might have something on your hands here. Something real special."

Later that day, when Valerie and I were over at Sheila's recruiting her to be our production designer, Meade called me there (it was my on-file home number at the college) to tell me I was all set with a production manager and a casting director to fill out the cast and extras.

Everything was working out beyond my greatest hopes. Then. Meade hit me with a slight buzz kill.

"And I did you one extra," he said with excitement.

"Oh?" I asked.

"I got you a male lead," he said. "This guy is the whole package, and the faculty over at the theater department loves him."

"But I have a male lead," I said. "Me."

"But you're not an actor," he said. "Not experienced or trained anyway. And trust me, as a first-time director, the last thing in the world you won't be dealing with is managing your own performance in the middle of blocking out the next setup."

I wanted to say *thank you very much, Professor Meade, but really, I'm all set with the male lead*. But what he would have heard was, *fuck you very much, Meade. Even after all you have just done for me, I am going to deny your boy a chance at his big break because I am an ungrateful bastard*.

Before he retreated to the safe confines of academia, Professor Meade was a working director and quite successful. He directed over fifty episodes of TV dramas and a handful of low to modest budget movies, mostly arthouse fare. It was clear he still thought and operated like someone still in the business because, in fact, what he was doing here, was cashing in. He had done me a favor, securing me a production manager and casting. Now he wanted me to give his boy the lead. And if I said no, he could easily make another call or two and undo those favors he had done me earlier.

In some ways dealing with Hollywood people was just as bad as dealing with gangsters. But without the violence—most of the time anyway.

So I had no choice but to accept Professor Meade's offer.

"So, what's this guy's name?"

"Johnny Swell," he replied. "A stage name, obviously."

"Yeah, I kinda figured that," I said.

Johnny fucking Swell? Are you kidding me?

The cameras had not even been rented yet, but already felt like the film was being fucked.

But after I hung up the phone, I kept my frustration silent, not wanting to upset Valerie or Sheila. I had to maintain an air of supreme confidence.

No matter what, I had to make this work.

Because hanging over all of it, there was that cement shoes at the bottom of the Atlantic Ocean thing.

Chapter 11 – First Day of Shooting

Besides my jack-of-all-trades hard-working tireless production manager Cliff, the biggest score of the deal with Professor Meade was in the casting of the film's villain.

He was an accomplished and charismatic Latin theatrical actor named Richard Mendez—a brass tacks, let's get down to business, actor's actor. Not one for socializing. When we headed out as a group to get some dinner out on Biscayne Bay or drinks down in the Grove after a ball-busting fifteen hour day, Mendez was nowhere in sight. But on the set, he took my direction to a tee and nailed it every time on the first take. We had a terrific villain, and the scenes with him and Valerie in the final act were going to be awesome.

On the other hand, there was our male lead.

My introduction to Johnny Swell was not the disaster I had anticipated.

Sure, he was full of himself, but he was actually pretty good when we ran the lines in rehearsal. He was handsome and would photograph well. The chemistry with Valerie was flat. She was visibly disappointed at the last minute change in the male lead. But the repertoire between them could be developed. Bottom line, I was hopeful.

Then came the first day of shooting, and it all went to hell in a handbasket.

Due to financial and practical reasons, movies are almost never shot in sequence. Our opening pre-credit scene, where Amanda is killed in a water-skiing accident, was a complex (and expensive) scene with extra, boats, and stunts. It was going to be a pain in the ass, so I scheduled it last on the shoot to avoid any cost over-runs. Plus, it gave me time to figure out how to fake the actual accident and explosion. This wasn't a Hal Needham studio film. Doing that stunt for real would take our entire budget and then some. But I remembered seeing a low budget Eurotrash flick where all we saw was the explosion reflected in a close-up of a character's sunglasses. That I knew how to do, and it could make it look really cool by shooting it with some grainy high contrast Super 16 film stock that we could blow up to 35mm in the lab.

So for our first day of shooting, we would be covering all the permitted stuff in the Coconut Grove Plaza, including a big scene set inside the AMC movie theater. We end up there after our protagonist Jimmy gazes down from his office window and swears he sees someone who looks just like Amanda, his lost love that died do tragically in that boating accident ten years ago as they were celebrating their high school graduation. Captivated by what he has just seen, Jimmy heads down to the street, playing voyeur, as he obsessively tracks the Amanda look-alike.

The first set-up was that office scene, and it was simple—just A and B camera's cutting between long medium and close-up shots, mixed with POV shots of Jimmy looking down and seeing the Amanda look-alike walking up into the Coconut Grove. The stuff he was looking at, Amanda/Valerie walking down the sidewalk, could be shot tomorrow when we had a long lens to work with. We were literally renting out cameras and lenses by the hour to save money.

Back to today's first set-up. Like I said, simple.

But as we were preparing to call action, Johnny Swell was off in a corner, psyching himself up like he was about to do a big speech in King fucking Lear before a packed house. He held up filming for almost thirty minutes—thirty minutes we could not afford to lose.

Then, he started to tell Bobby Z, my camera operator, where to position the lens and began barking orders at the gaffers, telling them how he liked to be lit.

Most actors are flakes. That I could handle. But don't you ever come on to my set and try to take over directing. Do that to any established working director—or unestablished—and you will get punched in the face.

"Stop!" I yelled.

I fought hard to control my temper. I calmly took Johnny Swell aside, as not to embarrass him on the set, and explained to him very politely but firmly that, "Johnny. I am the director. You are the actor. Are we clear?"

"But in the theater…" he began to whine.

"Hey, this ain't the fucking theater," I said. "And don't ever talk to my cameraman or anybody on the lighting crew ever again. Ever!"

Then after finally getting the coverage—despite him fighting me every step of the way, we quickly moved to the next set-up. As we walked, I yet again calmly but firmly explained to him that we did not have time to waste.

"I'm an actor," he spewed with arrogance. "And this is how I work. I go at my own pace."

I was done. I really wanted to punch him in the face. But I held back.

"Well, not anymore, you don't," I said. "At least not on this film."

"What's that mean?" he cried.

"You're done. Off the movie. History."

"But you can't fire me," he whined. "My uncle gave me this part."

That explains it. This meathead was Meade's nephew.

But Meade was a real director. Once I explained to him what went down, despite the nepotism involved, the professor would understand. Some things are sacrosanct among directors.

The entire cast and crew watched as this petulant asshole challenged my authority as the director. I needed to assert my alpha status and do it in no uncertain terms. Without punching him in the face, of course.

I walked up close to Johnny Swell and stared him down.

"Get the fuck off my set. Now," I said. "Or I will beat the living shit out of you, right here, right now, in front of all these good people whose movie you are fucking with."

He turned white as a ghost, turned and scampered away, whining and bitching some more under his breath. But he was gone. Thank God. And we still had time left on our access to the plaza.

I turned to the cast and crew who had gathered behind me watching the events unfold.

"Okay, people, end of sideshow. And we have a mother fucking movie to make," I said. "Is everybody here with me? No more flakes or drama queens?"

They all laughed and roared back a "no!" in unison.

"Are you with me?" I asked again, but louder, using the same energetic wound up tone and body motions the coaches used to fire up our team during the drudgery of a hard practice.

And they responded with another unison roar lead by Bobby Z, Sharon, and my production manager Cliff.

Just to put an exclamation point on it, Bobby Z called out, "Fuck yeah! We're with you, boss!"

"Okay then," I said. "Let's do this."

I turned to Sharon and Cliff. If this was going to work, and it was going to work, I needed these two to be my unflappable workhorses, along with the always dependable Bobby Z.

"We will reshoot the office stuff upstairs at the end of the day since it's unoccupied anyway."

I turned next to Bobby Z, who was really looking comfortable in his role as the camera operator in charge of a team of gaffers. I saw a DP in the making with him. I made a mental note to talk to him about taking some cinematography classes at the U.

"While I get into wardrobe and makeup, let's set up for the one-shot tracking Steadicam of Valerie, with Jimmy following her up into the AMC. Just like we rehearsed it with the storyboards."

"I'm on it," Bobby said.

Then I turned to Valerie. She was absolutely glowing.

This was her time, and her movie, as much as it was mine. And my God, she looked ready for it.

"Come down to the wardrobe trailer while I change," I said, unable to conceal just how dirty that sounded.

"Really?" she said.

"We can run a few lines to get me warmed up," I said. "And maybe rehearse a bit for that kissing scene."

"Oh, I think we should hold off on that part," she said. "Let the tension build."

She ran the tips of her fingers up along the inside of my forearm, sending spasms of tingling pleasure quaking all over me.

"You tease," I said.

"Yes, but think about how real—and how hot it will be on film if you can capture all that bottled up lust," she whispered as we walked up to the wardrobe trailer.

"Indeed," I said.

And she was right. The rest of the day's shoot went off like a surreal dream, as I tracked the luminous and captivating Valerie/Amanda with the Panavision wide-angle lens mounted on the Steadicam, allowing the camera to play the role of lingering voyeur. For the next sequence, I seamlessly moved to a handheld camera, obsessively following her into the movie theater where *Nightmare on Elm Street: Dream Warriors* was playing on the matinee screen amid a theater with extras posing as movie patrons.

Then came the next setup. Outside the theater, underneath the staircase of the plaza where Amanda reveals to Jimmy that she knows he is following her—because she wanted him to.

Then, the big money shot. The kiss. And not just any kiss.

Back when I wrote the script and imagined the scene, I was determined this would be the absolute most epic kiss in the history of cinema. With blocking inspired by a scene from Brian De Palma's *Body Double*, I had Bobby Z and the Steadicam ever so gently move around us in a gradually accelerating circular pan as Valerie and me—in character as Amanda and Jimmy—kissed, caressed, groped, and made out in the most passionate, lustful, arousing, delicious spit-swapping, open-mouthed, deep kissing session and groping embrace in the history of cinema.

At least it sure felt that way. And I could not wait to see the dailies, because I knew it would look and feel just as visceral and hot on film.

After an inauspicious start, the first day of shooting turned out to be a smashing success. And as we wrapped the final set-up of the day, I knew something to be true. I knew it because I felt it in my soul.

This movie was going to work.

Chapter 12 – A Real Director at Last

The next twenty weeks swept by like a euphoric, blissful dream. I imagined it all playing out like the coolest montage music video sequence ever.

The shoot came in at twenty-seven days, three days ahead of schedule. With an average of ten complex set-ups per day, it was ball bursting work to be sure. But there was so much enthusiasm, it was like being part of a championship team. Everyone was into it, because hey, we were making a mother fucking movie, God dammit.

We were making magic.

I spent my days not only orchestrating the machinations of movie-making but being in character as my alter ego Jimmy, obsessing over a lost love that seemingly had returned to him from beyond the grave. I spent my nights at the Adventure by the Sea in Valerie's apartment overlooking the Atlantic Ocean, basking in the heated passions of a love affair that was every bit as improbable and obsessive. As the weeks of shooting went on, the lustful fire between Valerie and I only increased, as did the growing emotional bond between us.

We celebrated the official end of principle photography by going out as a cast and crew to see a sneak preview of Brian De Palma's new movie, The *Untouchables*, at the AMC near the Adventura Mall. Afterward, we at the Friday's next door, eschewing the trendy scenes at South Beach and the Grove, in favor of pure 80s Americana at its glorious, tackiest best. That night the bond between Valerie and I seemed to soar to new levels of physical and emotional intimacy as erotic, desperate fucking morphed with super-intense, almost supernatural love-making.

The shoot of *The Return of Amanda* had been such a dreamy affair, a real, live movie set where I was living out my adolescent daydreams on a daily basis. So it was inevitable there would be a bit of a letdown when the post-production began. It was a tedious process with none of the exhilarating rush of shooting on location or a set. After all, there was no Valerie around for me to linger over with my Panavision lens in the editing room, just her tiny image in the as we screened and studied the footage.

But post-production was half the deal. I had to get it right. The editing mix often it would make or break a film. So I chose my editor carefully, going to a veteran, seasoned pro named Edith Keeler, a UM faculty member, who gladly accepted once I offered her five points and showed her some dailies. As we hovered over the Moviola looking at the processed footage from the lab, she was impressed with the coverage.

"Great camera placement and movement," she said. "Strong visual choices and nice framing.

Edith promised she could mold the footage into a "super tight, taught, romantic mystery thriller."

Then, as late spring rolled into summer and the looming premiere date at the Coconut Grove Film Festival was fast approaching, I had one final key ingredient to deal with—the music.

Thanks to our speedy shooting schedule, getting freebies on wardrobe, some locations, and even catering, together with so many people willing to work for points, we had over ten grand left over for our music budget.

I loved the pop song *Don't Dream It's Over* by Crowded House. Thematically it fit, I had a perfect spot to place it in the film, and it's just an awesome song. Plus, I could cut a music video together for a trailer. I figured I was dreaming to think we would be able to afford the rights but had Sharon look into it anyway. They insisted on seeing the scene where I intended to use the song, so I made a VHS of it and sent it to them. And, son of a bitch, they let us have it—for free—provided I make a promotional music video, which of course, I had planned on anyway.

So I had the whole ten grand left over to put toward a score, not exactly enough to fund the multi-week session with the London Symphony Orchestra composed and conducted Pino Donaggio soundtrack I was hoping for. Or so I thought.

Once again, the Gods of the cinema smiled on us.

Sharon knew someone in the Roman Studies department who traveled back and forth to Italy once a month and knew Pino Donaggio's mother bleeping agent. No, really. It was insane. Even more insane was that he agreed to do it for ten grand and points in the movie and had the time with the orchestra all taken care of on his end. Since he was in Italy and spoke no English, there would literally be no collaboration. From what I had read in *Starlog*, this was the same way he had worked with Joe Dante on *Piranha* and *The Howling*. We would send a cut of the film to Italy with Sharon's contact. Four weeks later, we would get the score back—and my God what a score it was. A soaring, haunting musical opus of romantic suspense—just in time to add to our final post-production mix before we printed the Festival ready final cut.

Of course, during this whole process, from the blissful shoot to the productive post-production, there was that one thorn in my side I had to deal with each week. One nagging reminder of the potential grim reality facing me if *The Return of Amanda* did not get some kind of sweet deal.

Every Sunday morning, I made the short trek across the Grove to Jerry's gaudy gangster mansion to meet with Charlie and deliver my weekly payment.

"Always on time and always paying in full," Charlie said. "My kind of client."

"But hey there, Mr. Spielberg, Just remember this," he cautioned. "Make sure you are just as punctual when it comes time to pay back that principal. September 1st is coming up fast. Real fast."

"Yeah, tell me about it," I said. "Tell your boss, no worries. He'll get his money."

Charlie laughed.

"Oh, trust me Hollywood, he ain't worried. That's my job," he said. "Just make sure I don't have to come looking for you."

On that ominous note, I left Charlie after making the payment— my last payment before the start of the festival.

The movie was ready. More than ready. Of that, I was sure.

But in any artistic field, no matter how much talent you have, no matter how hard you go at it, no matter how good the work might be, there that one factor, that one intangible that mattered more than anything.

Luck.

I prayed the Gods of Cinema would continue to bless our little film. And save my ass in the process.

Chapter 13 – The Festival

Here is how it read in the festival program and in the Miami Herald and The Fort Lauderdale Sun Sentinel:

The Coconut Grove Film Festival and AMC Theaters proudly present *The Return of Amanda*—a sensual, romantic, suspense thriller from Miami Studios starring the captivating newcomer Valerie Perry and featuring innovative and dazzling camera work from writer/director/cinematographer Rem Rasso.

That capsule summary was written by the Festival's staff, so I was hoping it was indicative of how they felt about the film. If the staff liked something, they would inevitability steer patrons and critics toward the screening. More asses in the seats. More potential votes. More exposure to producers and studio execs. Less of chance that my ass ended up in a canal somewhere in the Everglades or at the bottom of Biscayne Bay.

We scored a solid opening timeslot. Our premiere was to be on Sunday at 2 PM. Not as good as a Friday or Saturday opening. But far better than being stuck at the Festival's back end on Monday or Tuesday when all but the hardest of hardcore would be long gone.

But what happened on Friday was by far the most important thing that was going to happen.

The Return of Amanda made the first cut after being screened by the Festival's board, meaning it would be previewed for critics on either Tuesday or Wednesday. Which meant there would be a review in the Herald and Sun Sentinel in the Friday "weekend" section of the papers. Those reviews, particularly the one in the Miami Herald, would make or break us. The Herald's longtime, highly respected film critic, Bill Cosford, was notoriously tough to get a positive review from, and the Sun Sentinel's Candice Russel had a reputation as cineaste elitist. So I as I climbed out of the heavenly pleasure of Valerie's bed at the crack of dawn on Friday,

August the 7th, to head down to the lobby to grab a copy of both papers, I was understandably a nervous wreck.

The life of dreaming, the planning, the passion, spending years getting the script right, finding the dream lead, the gangster money, the hard work of the perfect shoot, lucking into an A-list composer—none of that meant anything right now because it all came down to the opinion of two people.

My life was literally in the hands of Bill Cosford and Candice Russell.

I inserted my quarters into each dispenser and got a copy of each newspaper. Then I took the papers with me over to a nearby bench in the lobby, sat down, and held my breath.

I opened the Miami Herald Weekend Section first—and I almost passed out.

The headline read:

Hypnotic 'The Return of Amanda' channels Hitchcock and De Palma

And the review began, "Writer/Director Rem Rasso's dazzling, sensuous The Return of Amanda showcases a strong debut performance Miami's own Valerie Perry in the title role. This stylish film stands as one of the best entries in the festival and should be factored in the big prizes, and a hit with audiences as well."

At the end of the positive, and at times glowing review, was the final verdict, ***1/2 stars out of four. Getting three stars from Bill Cosford was like pulling teeth. Getting three and half was fucking huge.

I peeked into the Sun Sentinel's Weekend Showtime Magazine to get another dose of good news. Shockingly, Candice Russell gave it three stars, and like Cosford, praised the direction, the score, and Valerie's performance.

This was huge. This was fucking epic.

I went upstairs to share the good news with Valerie, and we celebrated by furiously and lustfully attacking each other before sitting down to a breakfast of homemade (with the help of

Bisquick) blueberry pancakes. Afterward, we showered and dressed in our best—Valerie in a clinging black femme fatale dress and me in a standard director jeans, running sneakers, a t-shirt with our *The Return of Amada* poster art, and a baseball cap with the *Miami Studios* logo on it.

Then, we headed down to the parking lot, climbed into the 5.0, and drove down to the Coconut Grove AMC to meet up with the rest of the cast and crew for our big coming-out party at the Festival.

The next three days were a public relations whirlwind of backslapping, handshakes, and intense one on one selling.

Oh, the potential buyers of the film were there to be sure. Lots and lots of them from every production company and studio, both big and small. But it all depended on Sunday's screening. Cosford and Russell's reviews were just step one. That would get them into the theater. So there would be asses in the seats. But how would they react? Would they like the film? Enough to commit a small fortune to it?

It all came down to that Sunday screening. Yikes.

Valerie and I were there an hour early to warm the patrons up with my film geek enthusiasm and her knockout femme fatale glamorous charms. Bobby Z was there to talk about our creative crane shots—thanks to the local fire department. And Sharon worked the crowd, displaying an impressive blend of marketing savvy and take charge of Hollywood style leadership. I told her and everyone else that she was the next Kathleen Kennedy or Gale Anne Hurd.

Even our villain, the anti-social Richard Mendez, was there for our big make or break moment. And finally, after a near-capacity crowd of about 175 movie insiders, critics, and hardcore film nuts settled down into their seats, the lights dimmed, the theater went dark, and the projector hummed to life.

I held my breath, then forced myself to take in air so as not to pass out. I felt Valerie's heavenly skin brush up against mine as she clasped my hand and held tight.

The next ninety-eight minutes were like a bizarre and surreal out of body experience. Like seeing the most personal parts of your life and your deepest dreams projected on a giant, larger than life canvas in front of group of strangers, who sat in the dark ready to judge, not just your work, but the very essence of your soul.

But in the end—when the credits began to roll—I could only hear one overwhelming noise.

The intoxicating sounds of exhilaration.

Applause. Cheers. Back slapping. Handshakes and hugs.

The Return of Amanda became the smash hit of the Coconut Grove Film Festival 1987.

Chapter 14 – The After Party

Vestron made the first offer at six-hundred thousand. Lionsgate leap-fogged that to seven-hundred fifty thousand. Then Dimension decided to get serious at nine-hundred grand.

Several other entities chimed in on the bidding, including freaking Paramount Pictures. But at the end of the day, it was Dino De Laurentiis Studios who took the cake at one point two million.

"This movie will make a killing in Europe," the producer from Dino De Laurentiis said. "It will play well everywhere. Very Giallo. Dino will love this."

Translation. Everybody with points scored—big time.

As the lead—and the true and only reason the movie worked—I gave Valerie forty points. That was four-hundred eighty grand. Ten points for Sharon and the Maestro Pino Donaggio, that's one-hundred twenty grand each. Five points to the editor Edith Keeler, Production Manager Cliff, cousin Sheila, and my man Bobby—sixty grand each.

That left twenty points or two hundred forty grand for me. I did not need two forty. Just one fifty to pay Jerry, and say another twenty to make sure I had rent and food money till my next directing gig. So that left seventy grand. I spread out fifty among the gaffers, the caterers, the AMC manager, and a bunch of other unsung heroes who helped the movie get made. The last twenty grand I split between the local chapter of the Humane Society from where Val had adopted Tommy and a conservation group dedicated to saving the Florida panther.

It was all falling into place. I just had one last task to perform. A trip into that gaudy mansion in the heart of Coconut Grove to get Jerry Strombolo out of my life once and for all. I offered to do the same for Valerie. Take half of her Amanda money and buy him out, end of story, full stop. But Val insisted on handling that herself.

I knew this was a potentially volatile situation, even though it should be a simple, straightforward deal. I knew that because I was dealing with a volatile man. So I bit the bullet and brought an extra ten grand of my twenty remaining for savings as a sweetener. Just to make sure this fucker would let me walk away quietly.

When I reached the front gate, I was not greeted by Charlie as per the norm. Instead, one of the thick-necked guards said, "He wants to see you inside."

By he, I assumed he meant Jerry. I had a bad feeling about this.

Once inside, I was led by another guard into the dining room with all of the mounted TVs—the same room I was in during that first fateful visit here.

Jerry entered, chomping a cigar and wearing a long sleeve purple silk shirt about two sizes too small for his corpulent girth. Charlie was right behind him, looking characteristically sharp, but also very uncharacteristically nervous.

"So I understand our movie was a big mother fucking hit," Jerry quipped.

What the fuck did he mean by *our movie*?

Now I really, really, had a bad feeling about this.

"I understand you got something there for me, Hollywood?" Jerry said.

I took out the fat envelope stuffed with the cash and handed it to him.

"That's the full amount of one-hundred fifty grand," I said. "Plus an extra ten grand. Just to show my appreciation."

Jerry tossed the envelope down on the table and took the cigar out of his mouth.

"What the fuck?" Jerry said. "I own half the movie. Ain't that what you told me, Hollywood? So you owe my six-hundred grand. Ain't that right, Charlie?"

Charlie said nothing.

I should have tried to keep my cool. But like I said earlier, I have that temper issue. And I really don't like being gaslit. And I really, really, don't like anyone fucking with movie.

So I talked to Jerry, not like some petrified civilian who'd cave in to his bullying shenanigans. But instead, I looked him in the eyes and talked to him like some other gangster would if Jerry was trying to lie and cheat them.

"What the fuck are talking about, Jerry?" I said. "You turned down that offer."

"Oh? You calling me a liar?" Jerry said.

"Yeah, I'm calling you a liar," I said. "

"You said, and I quote, *I only bet on sure things*," I continued. "So instead, you loaned me the money in the same way you would loan it out to anyone in the street. And everybody in this room, including Charlie and Rocko and Moose here, along with Valerie, heard both you and I specifically agree and to the stated terms of two percent a week interest and principal payment of the one-hundred-fifty grand on September 1st."

I turned to Charlie.

"Charlie, did I or did I not honor those exact terms?" I asked.

"You did," Charlie said.

Jerry gave him a look of murderous rage.

"Look at you? Think you get to tell me what to do? You think you get to tell me anything? Well there, Hollywood. Mister Slick. Guess what?" he said. "I'm changing the terms. You owe be six-hundred grand."

I just shook my hood.

"You know Jerry, you are a real piece of work," I said. "And the tragedy of all of this is you could have had that six-hundred grand. If you just had the balls to take a fucking risk. Instead of betting on, you know, sure things."

Jerry looked like he was going to explode. I half expected a physical attack and quickly thought about the fastest way to put him down if he came at me. But the reason Jerry had all those goddamn guards was that he did not like to do the actual fighting himself. So he just called out to either Moose or Rocko.

"Richie, blow this cocksucker's head off, right now!" Jerry screamed.

Richie looked hesitant. Thankfully, before he could make a decision in Jerry's favor, Charlie interceded, standing in the middle of us like a referee stopping a potential fight during a basketball game.

"Now. Let's all just cool down," Charlie said.

He turned to Jerry and spoke to Jerry in a soothing but firm voice.

"I'll talk to him," Charlie said. "I'll take care of this."

Then, Charlie came to my side, keeping his cool, and started to escort me toward the front door. As we exited the house, Jerry's words echoed after us.

"Well, you'd better take care of this and get me my fucking money, Charlie. Or it'll be your head getting blown off too!"

And with that, Charlie walked me out to the car and sent me off with the none-too-reassuring words of, "Don't worry. "I'll talk to him."

"What? Me worry?" I remarked. "Just some gangster threatening to blow my head off. Why in God's name would I worry about that?"

As Charlie headed inside to try and reason with a psychopath, I drove back up to Adventura to update Valerie. And to warn her away from even thinking about approaching Jerry.

"That's who he is," Valerie said. "A lying piece of shit. A real menace."

She took the news of my encounter with Jerry with surprising stride. With too much stride. When I pressed her on it, she said she had faith in Charlie.

"He'll handle Jerry. So I don't want you worrying," she said.

"This is your time, Rem. And I will not let that fucker take this away from you. I promise you that, sweetie."

She held me close, clinging to me in an emotionally vulnerable way she had never done before. She felt so good, and I now felt closer to her than ever.

"So what you want to do tonight?" I asked. "South Beach? The Grove? Dinner on Key Biscayne?"

She paused for a moment as if thinking about it, then looked at me with an intense, romantic gaze.

"No, none of those," she said. "Tonight, I want to be like a normal couple."

"As opposed to a super chic, trendy, Miami slash Hollywood style couple?" I asked.

"Exactly," she said.

"Well, as someone who used to be one of those normal types, I know exactly what's in order," I said.

"Oh?" she said.

"We go down to AMC right here in Adventura and see *Dirty Dancing*," I said. "I hear it's already shaping up to be the sleeper hit of the year."

"Yes!" she said, lighting up. "Then we go to Friday's afterward and pig out on loaded up potato skins."

"Bingo!" I said.

She held me tight again, gently caressing my face and neck with that perfect touch of hers, with those perfect hand model fingertips.

"I want tonight to be just us," she said. "A normal couple. A real couple. A forever couple."

Then she kissed me in a wanton, tender, and desperate way, unlike any way she had ever kissed me before.

The entire night—the movie, the dinner, the love-making at home afterward, really was unlike anything before. We really were like a normal couple. A real couple. A forever couple. I felt like I was living a fairytale romantic comedy. One destined to have the wonderful happy ending that sends your heart soaring during as the closing credits roll, and a sentimental pop tune blasts out over the Dolby speakers.

That night I forgot all about Jerry. And I slept more deeply and peacefully than I had ever before in my life.

But when I awoke the next morning, there was a note sitting on the nightstand near the bed, and it all came crashing down.

It was a Dear John letter of a very different sort.

It read:

Rem,

I am so sorry to write you like this. But there was just no other way.

I could no longer take living under the thumb of that monster. He took my business form me. He took my best friend from me. And now, he is threatening to take you from me, and I can never let that happen. Trust me when I tell you he will never stop. He will steal your life just like he has mine. There is only one way to stop a menace like Jerry Strombolo. And you know what that is.

Don't worry about me. I'll get in. Give him what he deserves. And get out. I'll have help on both ends. Turns out his bodyguards are sick and tired of the mood swings, the petulance, and the cruelty. They hate him as much as everyone else. The only thing I can't control is the video cameras. Among other things, Jerry is a paranoid psychopath. Even the guards don't know where every camouflaged camera is and hidden VCRs are. So in all likelihood, everyone, from the local PD to that wretched family in NYC, will know it was me. That means I have to disappear and stay disappeared for a very long time.

Now here comes the hard part. The agonizing part. The part that is breaking my heart. Saying good-bye to you.

Rem, these last six months—that life-altering moment when I spotted you across the patio at Sheila's party, that action-packed first date on South Beach, that first day of shooting, the premier at the film festival—I mean, I starred in a freaking movie because of you! I feel like I lived a lifetime like we lived a whole life together in such a short time. Such was the intensity of our passion and our love. These past six months have meant everything to me, Rem. Because you mean everything to me.

Love always,
Val

It was a vicious punch in the gut. I felt panic. Like I could not breathe. A mix of overwhelming emotions was swirling inside me.

Anger, because she did not come to me first to try and figure out a better way out of this. Satisfaction, because Jerry Strombolo really was, as Valerie said, a menace, and he finally got what was coming to him. Appreciation, because Valerie really did make this life-altering sacrifice to protect me as much as to get herself from under that fat prick's hovering presence. But most of all, I just felt an aching sense of emptiness. Valerie was it for me. She was my Amanda. And now I wondered with a heavy heart if I would ever see her again.

Of course, as I was there in the apartment reeling as if on cue, there was a knock on the door. It was Charlie. And this time, he actually came alone.

I was not in the mood.

"Yes, I know. And no, I don't know where she is or where she is going," I said in an effort to cut off any interrogation.

"And I can show you the note she left me to prove it," I added.

"Hey, Spielberg. Relax," he said calmly. "Your girl did not just save your ass. She did us all a big favor. You don't know how many times I came close to slitting that fat fucker's throat myself."

"He was an abusive asshole. Even his personal bodyguards were happy," he said. "They let Valerie walk right out of there and did so gladly."

"Yeah, she mentioned that in the note," I said.

"So everybody is happy this piece of shit is gone," I said. "Does that mean Val can come out of hiding?"

"Absolutely not," Charlie said. "The cops will have something to say about that. I don't own all of them. Jerry may be hated and was exiled down here for a reason, but he still has a few loyalists up in New York. Including a brother who's more of a psycho than he is. And mean."

"So if Val ever does contact you—and I doubt she will because she would never want to put you in harm's way—you tell her to stay lost," Charlie added. "Hopefully, on some tropical island, far, far, away."

"She okay with money?" he asked.

"Yeah," I said. "Points in the movie."

"Then, don't worry. She'll be fine," Charlie said. "Val's smart as a whip. And very resourceful."

I nodded, trying to fight back the realization that, indeed, I might never see her again.

I tried to shake the suffocating melancholy by focusing on Charlie.

"So, does this mean you're the big cheese now?" I asked.

"They'll have to send down someone. Probably one of the Boss's coke-snorting vapid nephews. A figurehead," he said. "But yeah, I'll be running Miami."

Charlie took an envelope out of his jacket and tossed it to me.

"What's this?" I asked.

"That extra ten grand you tried to give Jerry. You know, just to make sure what happened didn't happen," he said. "Don't ever try to placate an asshole. It only makes them more of an asshole."

"Lesson learned," I said.

I tossed the envelope back to Charlie.

"Keep it," I said. "Consider it my parting gift to you and your new administration. No offense, Charlie, I like you and all. But I really want to put this whole gangster storyline part of my life behind me. Like, forever."

Charlie smiled and put the envelope back in his jacket.

"Fair enough," he said.

He went to leave. But before he opened the door, he turned back to face me.

"But I do have one condition," he said.

"Oh?" I asked, holding my breath.

"Lou Gossett Jr.," he said.

"What?" I asked.

"If you ever make a movie about this part of your life, I want to be played by Lou Gossett Jr.," he said.

"Charlie, consider it done," I said.

I met with the manager of Adventura by the Sea to explain that Valerie would be on an extended sabbatical, and I would be taking over the lease. Then, I updated Sheila on my situation to have her come by and apartment sit, and take care of Tommy when I was away working on a film or TV show, which I was hoping would be more often than not.

Turned out that Dino De Laurentiis and company made a killing on their investment in *The Return of Amanda.* They were right about the European markets.

The movie made over forty million internationally and twenty-two million domestically. That got me a CAA agent and multiple directing offers, including a bunch to direct episodes of TV shows, including *Tales from the Dark Side,* and the new *Twilight Zone,* which had just moved from CBS to syndication. But it was the offer from Paramount that intrigued me the most.

"A twelve million dollar budget. Enough to get big names and cool toys," the Exec said, gushing with enthusiasm. "Not to mention, cool sets and great locations."

"You'll have card blanche," he said. "Except for a few things. Some items we do require. You know."

"Actually, I don't," I said, having a flashback to me dealing with Jerry. "So how about you spell it out. In precise detail."

The Exec was unflappable as he continued his pitch.

"We want something in the same mode as *The Return of Amanda*, sexy, mysterious, suspenseful, haunting, with supernatural overtones."

"Okay," I said. "I can manage that. What else."

"A strong female character lead. Like *Amanda*," he said. "And we absolutely love Valerie Perry. She is magnificent and carried your film and is going to be a huge star one day. But to justify this budget, we need current stars. We were thinking Ellen Barkin— have you seen *The Big Easy*? Or Kim Basinger. I mean *9 1/2 Weeks*. Hello. And for the male, maybe Jeff Bridges or Kevin Costner or…but hey, listen, we really do like Valerie, and we thought maybe you could write a strong secondary character for her?"

My mind began to drift off into a wanton haze, the images of Valerie flashing by, flickering alive as if it were a Super 8 film being projected inside my mind.

"She's….currently unavailable," I said.

"That's too bad. Maybe on the next film," he said. "Back to the male lead…"

As the Exec rambled on, I knew I would take this deal.

I would take this movie. And I would make this movie about Valerie. The woman who, upon one glance at a backyard party from across the patio, had captured my lust, my heart, and my imagination, and would own them forever.

She was my Amanda.

She was my everything.

Bonus Short Story

Jennifer the Sketchbook Girl

James J. Caterino
FANTASTIC
JC
2020
Jennifer the Sketchbook Girl

Jennifer the Sketchbook Girl

James J. Caterino

Other works by James J. Caterino include:

Fantastic Stories: Season 2 (2020)
Femme Fatales: The Art of James J. Caterino (2020)
The Girl from the Stars (2019)
Fantastic Stories (2019)
Fireflies (2018)
Caitlin Star: The Trilogy (2016)

Chapter 1 – Jennifer's World

The bell sounded, indicating the end of the hour. Jennifer sat for a moment at her desk, slowly packing up her things, as the rest of the class scattered to the exits of the auditorium, in a seeming rush to get wherever it was they were going.

Jennifer was different from the others. For them, this was no doubt just something they had to do to notch fulfillment one of their art and sciences requirements. But for Jennifer, Professor Rhodes' philosophy class was something she looked forward to every Monday, Wednesday, and Friday afternoon. And today's subject was something she found utterly fascinating—determined fate vs. free will.

Walking out of the auditorium and into the bright daylight of the South Florida North Miami Dade Community College campus, she decided to catch up with Dr. Rhodes, to try and pick his brain. It took more time and effort than she had anticipated. Dr. Rhodes was a known and accomplished 5K runner and his walk was akin to a sprint for most people

"Dr. Rhodes," she said, trying to catch her breath as he turned and matched stride with her.

"Jennifer," he said with his usual beaming smile. Dr. Rhodes was one of the few professors she ever had who was not always consistently approachable, but always in a good mood.

"What can I do for you?" he asked.

"I have a question for you," she said.

"And that is exactly what makes you an excellent student," he said. "You question things. You push the boundaries. I like that. Keeps me motivated to teach."

She took a moment to soak in the compliment.

It felt good to hear that. To be taken seriously. That was difficult to do because of the way she looked. She was, or so people told her, very pretty—a "knockout," they said. Most men could not get past that. And most women hated her for it.

Plus, just the fact that she was female. Sure, it was 1987, and things had changed for the better. But still, as she was reminded every day, especially by the obnoxious shop boss at the truck rental agency where she worked, this was still a man's world.

"Jennifer?" Dr. Rhodes said, prompting her to get out of her head and onto the question.

"Oh, yes," she said. "That was what I wanted to ask about. The pushing boundaries thing."

"In what way?" he asked.

"Well…it's just that I've been reading a lot of Phillip K Dick in the science fiction class I'm taking for the English/Lit credit," she said.

She could see Dr. Rhodes' eyes light up.

"Ahh, yes!" he said. "He kind of blows your mind with all that nature of reality stuff."

"Yes, exactly!" she said.

"What if…what if he were on to something," she said. "What if, this…all this stuff around us is like a microcosm? A mini-bubble universe within some far greater reality beyond what we can see. What if there was a way to break those…boundaries…and gain access to it."

"For the world is hollow and I have touched the sky," he said.

"Yes, exactly," Jennifer said. "What is that? From a poem or something."

"It's the title of a third season *Star Trek* episode," he said.

Dr. Rhodes stopped his sprinting walk stride, turned to her, shook his head, and smiled gently.

"Keep in mind, Phillip K. Dick did a lot of LSD," he said. "He was brilliant, yes. Had a great imagination and was a good storyteller. But he was crazier than a bed bug."

Jennifer felt deflated.

Yeah, maybe he was on drugs when he wrote that stuff and was bat shit crazy. But Phillip K. Dick was on to something. She knew it.

"Jennifer," Dr. Rhodes said as they departed. "You think too much. And that is coming from a philosophy professor."

Chapter 2 – The Stalker

Mondays were Brutal for Jennifer.

Not just for all the standard reasons that Mondays were dreaded by almost any working stiff who endured the rigors of a job they hated because they needed the dough. For Jennifer, Mondays were extra sucky because she had to open the South Side branch of the Carlton Truck Rental location off of State Road 84 in Davie, Florida. Opening, as in be ready to open at 7 AM.

Well, at least she had her philosophy class to look forward to later today. Maybe she could try again to talk with Dr. Rhodes after class and try to convince him that Phillip K. Dick may have been crazy, but he also may have been right.

She cleared her head and prepped the counter, preparing for the inevitable customer onslaught as people returned their weekend rentals. But first, she had to deal with stress of a different kind.

She felt a nervous pit of anxiety well up in her stomach as Mike Drithers slithered into the store from a side door that connected to the shop.

Drithers was the head mechanic in the shop. He was loud, obnoxious, full of himself, and just an all-around first-grade asshole. And now, he had become Jennifer's stalker.

She made the mistake of being manipulated into betting with him on last year's Miami-FSU game. So, as a result of losing the bet, she had to endure lunch with him down at the roadside diner. It was lunch from a bet, "not a date," she had stressed. But to the sociopathic narcissist that was Mike Drithers, it may as well been a marriage proposal.

He saw it as a victorious conquest and had been in her face ever since—especially on the days when she opened and was there alone. It was as if he saw himself as entitled to her, and if he kept coming after her, she'd eventually wear down and give in.

"What? You don't answer your phone?" he said, leaning up into the counter as she organized the rental forms.

"I tried calling you all day on Saturday," he snapped.

She had never given him her phone number. He had gotten it
out of her employee file. When she complained to human
resources about that—and about the harassment—the old shrew
who ran the department looked at Jennifer with deep disdain.

"Well, maybe you should try dressing more conservatively," the
old shrew said.

Yeah? Well, fuck you, lady!

Of course, Jennifer did not actually say that. She needed this
job. At least for now. So—at least for now—she felt trapped.

"Jennifer, I asked you a question," Drithers said with a tone of
escalating anger.

Then he bent his large, slovenly form over the counter as if he
were about to try and put his mouth to hers and grope her.

"Why are you so rude to me?" he said.

The door chime sounded off as a group of costumers walked in.
Thank God.

Jennifer survived both her dickhead stalker's attempt to intimidate her and the Monday morning customer counter rush when she overheard her manager talking on the phone behind her.

It was the name she heard Dee spoke that grabbed her attention. The name of Jimmy Barton.

"He'll be here after lunch? Around one?" Dee was saying into the phone. "No problem. The truck's already checked in. It will be waiting for him."

Jennifer had first spotted Jimmy Barton while she was up at the Pompano Office on a supply run. And when she crossed paths with him in the tight quarters up the upstairs hallway there, she just about died.

The build. The curly hair. The teddy bear brown eyes. The presence. The inviting way he smelled. And that smile—my God that beaming smile. It was so overwhelming that she felt herself have a physical reaction while she fought to stay calm and manage an awkward "hello" as she stared at him dreamily.

It was love at first sight. Or at least a very, very intense crush. Far beyond anything she had felt before.

She had thought about, daydreamed about, and fantasized about Jimmy Barton every day since then.

Oh, she tried to play it cool. She didn't want to be a stalker like the creepy Drithers. But she was too emotional, too animated, too expressive, too bubbly, and too effervescent to keep her percolating feelings bottled up inside.

So she tried to make up any excuse she could to go up to the Pompano office in the hope of a Jimmy Barton sighting. She even confessed her feelings to Jimmy's temporary boss Traci. Temporary because Jimmy was freshly recruited out of college for the company's Management Trainee program. That meant he'd spent X amount of time at Pompano under Traci. Then X amount of time at a branch retail counter (South Side she prayed). Then, he would go on to manage a location somewhere or go to the corporate office in Miami and be on the fast track to the top.

Rock star charisma, built like an action hero, Hollywood Handsome, and a smart college boy—Jennifer was certain that a bright future laid ahead for Jimmy Barton. She certainly had good taste in men, even though she only seemed to attract the low-life assholes like Drithers. The drunks, the woman abusers, the downright scumbags of the male population. She was always in their crosshairs.

Maybe meeting Jimmy Barton was a sign her luck was about to change. But beyond the superficial and the biography, what was he like? She followed up with Traci to dig deeper and find out more.

It turned out he was a nice guy. "Super sweet," in Traci's words.

It sounded like Traci just adored him and had a lot of fun working with him, as they spent much of their non-busy time (something unique to back offices she surmised) talking about movies. Turns out, Jimmy wrote movie reviews for his college paper and went to the theater twice a week minimum.

It just kept getting better and better. And to add fuel to the fire, when Jennifer managed to arrange to pass him by in the close quarters of the Pompano office a second time, it confirmed something she had picked up on during that first fabled encounter.

He was just as attracted to her.

The chemistry between them was electric.

This was like something out of one of those movies Traci and Jimmy talked about in their downtime. This could be a real-life romantic comedy for Jennifer. The R rated kind with lots of hot sex and a happy ending. Maybe her luck really was about to change. Maybe, bringing it back to Dr. Rhodes' philosophy class, perhaps this was fated to be. Maybe they—Jennifer and Jimmy together—were fated to be.

If only…

Because there were two barriers to making that happen. One was easy to overcome. The second, so impossible, it was almost certainly a deal-breaker.

There was the age thing. Jennifer was eighteen. A freshman in her first fall semester of college and Jimmy was twenty-two, having just graduated out of college this past spring.

So, in a sense, they were both class of '87, right? And those four years meant nothing, right? At least that was what Jennifer told herself. But she knew that those four years might be meaningless down the road. But at this time and this age, it would all depend on him.

Though she was a mature eighteen as she was forced to grow up fast because of a home situation of an absent father and a mother with what Jennifer liked to say were "issues." This was all backstory that would not matter if Jimmy was someone who would hear "barely legal" when he heard eighteen and head for the exit.

Still, she had a good feeling this barrier would not be a problem.

The second one, well, that was something different.

Traci dealt her a near-fatal blow when she told Jennifer that Jimmy Barton had a fiancé.

But near-fatal was the keyword. Because there was just something about him. And something about that situation that she imagined it not being as final as it sounded.

Engagements end all the time, especially for couples at such a young age. Traci herself happened to leave her fiancé, literally standing at the aisle, two years ago. Ironically, that jilted ex was now the manager of the Pompano branch downstairs from the back office where Traci worked, and the two of them were very close friends.

Things happened. And right now, Jennifer had a feeling something big was about to happen. Something spectacular. Something fateful.

She began to think about the questions she would ask Dr. Rhodes later today at her philosophy class when the door chime sounded a swarm of customers stampeded in. She began checking them in when the doorbell chimed again, and in he came, backlit from behind by the streaming sunlight on his curly brown hair, as if he were making a major character in that epic romantic Jennifer imagined herself living in.

It was Jimmy Barton.

"Yes," she thought. "Something big was about to happen. Something amazing."

Chapter 3 – Dystopian Future

The COVID-19 quarantine was finally getting to Jimmy Barton.

He took pride in being a bit of a recluse. As a writer, it somehow seemed fitting. He hated most people and the human species in general. But this—this new endless era of social distance and isolation—this was somehow different.

Truth be told, for the first time in his five and half decades on this Earth, Jimmy Barton was lonely.

He had no family. His parents were long gone, and his siblings scattered about the country. But there were things that he missed. Things that he took for granted before because even though he was a loner, he never was alone before. Not really.

He went to the movies twice a week. Three times when the Herald gave him passes to an advanced screening and asked him to write a review.

He went to the gym almost every day, and he did have friends there in the gym rat sense of the word.

Every weekend, he would browse bookstores and comic book shops amid other like-minded book worms and four colors crack addicts.

Sometimes he would even meet up with one of the few humans he did actually like to catch up over lunch or dinner.

Then there was that thing he did every Saturday night. His sojourn to one of the high-end South Florida strip clubs.

He did not date anyone for all the usual reasons (it was just too damn complicated and too damn hard to find someone that was available, that he was attracted to, and that was not insane). But he needed physical contact, specifically with females that he really was attracted to. And the women at these clubs were very attractive, and they did touch you all over and in all the right ways.

It was what it was.

But man, did he really miss that touch right now.

He missed all of it—the movies, the gym, the bookstores, the comic book shops, the beautiful women touching him.

So he did the only thing he could to take the edge off the loneliness and the cravings. He threw himself obsessively into his new project—a project called *1987.*

Everyone has that one year in his or her life, that one special and horrific and magical year where a lifetime of living takes place. That one year that ends up being so much more consequential, so much more exhilarating, and so much more terrifying than all of the other years of life combined.

For Jimmy Barton, that year was 1987. It was a year that mattered in all the ways that counted. It was a year that forged a path into the future from which there could be no retreat.

1987 started with him graduating early and with honors from Carnegie Mellon University where he had played football for four years on a scholarship (being from what was then called a "mill hunky" working-class family, there was no other way he would have been able to afford to attend a school such as CMU).

His degree was in mechanical engineering, only because back then, that was the expected thing to do if you had the chance to get an education—be doctor, a lawyer, or an engineer. Anything remotely having do with that the "arts" (Jimmy's true interest was creative writing and film) was met with disapproving scowls among the practical-minded, hard-working folk of Western Pennsylvania circa 1983 (the year Jimmy started college). Or as his father used to say. "A Liberal arts degree? You might as well use that to wipe your ass."

So, he took as many writing and film electives as he could while laboring to get that degree in mechanical engineering. But his true major, as was the case with almost anyone who played the game at the college level, was football.

But Jimmy was different than most because he was actually good. Really good. He was a running back who rushed for over six thousand yards in four years, scored eighty-seven touchdowns, and made NCAA Division III All-American first team three years in a row.

He could block like a guard, catch like a tight end, and despite being from a Division III school, had garnered the attention from several NFL scouts, including one from the Miami Dolphins who invited him down to South Florida for a tryout in March.

So, 1987 sure started out like gangbusters for Jimmy. But there is another part of the story because when he ventured to relocate to Miami after graduation, he was not alone. He had a fiancé named Phoebe. That part of the story was complicated. Complicated because, in fact, he was not in love with her. Not a bit.

She had come to him, offering support in exactly the way he needed at the time. She did to him what was referred to in sales as "the assumptive close." And he went along with it because she was attractive and she was nice, to a point.

But most of all, it was just convenient. It was nice to have her in the way his degree in Mechanical Engineering was nice to have. He could no more have turned her advances away than he could have refused to accept his diploma at graduation time.

So, before he knew it, he was engaged, even though it was never his idea or even his intention.

Phoebe's parents were rich and connected, so she was set up at a prestigious, elite corporate Miami Law firm while he prepared for his tryout with the Dolphins.

On the long car ride down to Miami, Jimmy tweaked his back, and as the tryout date loomed closer, he was still tight back there. To make matters worse, he strained a hamstring while training—a week before his workout before the Dolphin coaches.

Hampered by the injuries and unable to showcase his trademark speed and explosiveness, the tryout was a disaster, dashing his dreams of playing in the same backfield as Dan Marino.

He married Phoebe in November, and that did not fare much better. Her controlling tendencies (and her parents) got increasingly worse. When he was told he was not allowed to buy comic books or go to the gym anymore ("you're not a kid, and football's over, so there is no need to go to the gym," she scolded), he knew that was it. The marriage was officially dissolved less than a year later (her father's influence over the judge was a plus, in this case, saving him the money and hassle of a divorce with an easy annulment).

But there was a casualty from his short time with Phoebe. The casualty of a lost love that never was named—Jennifer.

Jennifer was the subject of this new epic project, a graphic novel entitled *1987*.

Jennifer was the inspiration.

She was the star.

And he didn't even know her last name.

Because at the time, he did everything in his power to keep a safe distance from her and try to not even think about her. Because deep down, he knew the truth, even though he wouldn't admit it to himself at the time.

This Phoebe thing was a monstrous mistake.

And it was this beacon of school girl sweetness atop a boundless magnet of simmering sensuality—it was this goddess named Jennifer—this extraordinary larger than life vessel of beauty and charisma and goodness mixed with sultry badness in a good kind of way. This eighteen-year-old femme fatale who had rocked his world and made him feel things he never even knew existed. She was the one he was supposed to be with, and every time he gazed at her or grazed past her in the corridors of Carlton Truck Rental, it was confirmed by the insane chemistry he felt and re-confirmed by the heart-stopping surge of wanting love and unquenchable lust woven deep in his flesh and bones.

She was his destiny. She was fate

But a fate and destiny that was never to be.

1987—the year itself—ended.

As did his time at Carlton Truck Rental Company.

And by the time he was free of the chains of Phoebe, in the summer of 1988, the window had closed.

For a while, he kept in touch with one of his mentors at Carlton, a wonderful girl named Traci, who had been his boss. One day, he casually asked her about Jennifer, and her reply smacked him like a kick in the balls with a steel-toed construction boot.

Jennifer was now engaged to be married to some dipshit from the Carlton South Side shop named Mike—a beer-guzzling, obnoxious, loud-mouth dildoe who was, on top of everything else, ten years her senior.

He feared for her future. And mourned for his own.

A future without the one girl who had stirred something deep inside him. That special something that poets write about and singers sing for.

That 1987.

That was all a long, long time ago.

He had long ago lost touch with his last link from that era, Traci, and every attempt to find her online had come up short. She was a very private person—someone who would hate social media. He'd never be able to find her, let alone find out what happened to Jennifer. So he felt lost. As if that time and place and all those people were gone—lost to him forever. Vanished into the forgotten annals of time. An erased past that he could never reclaim.

Yes, it was all so long ago, and he should move on and forget about it. But now, thanks to COVID-19 and the endless quarantine and the desperate loneliness, it literally was all he could think about. It was making him mad, in the raving lunatic mad kind of way. How he longed for 1987. How he longed for *her*.

He had to make things right.

He had to find a way back to Jennifer. He had to find a way to tell her how he felt about her. And there was only one way to do all that.

He made some more story notes in a yellow legal pad on the table before him. He cleared his mind and pictured Jennifer until he could remember every vivid detail about her as if it were yesterday. He could even remember her insanely seductive smell.

Then he opened up his sketchbook, took out a 2B pencil, and began to draw.

He would bring 1987 back.

He would rewrite the past with a pencil, pen, and ink.

He would finally be with his long-lost love and the girl of his dreams.

1987 and Jennifer would live again.

With her glorious, radiant, larger than life image bursting alive in his mind, Jimmy locked into the creative zone and began to draw her.

First, he selected a pose, a stance he remembered her taking during a company picnic in June of 1987 for the roaming photographer gathering shots for the company newsletter, the same newsletter he wrote weekly movie reviews for.

He remembered that picnic and that pose in vivid, hyper-real, cinematic detail. He remembered the denim shorty-shorts and the open-toed sandals and the *Fantastic Stories* t-shirt she wore that day, and how superbly it clung to the sculpted contours of her body, a glorious form that managed to be both femme fatale and athletic at the same time.

He remembered how she leaned into the camera, offering the peace sign. He remembered those lips, lips that begged and pleaded to be kissed, and those expressive, animated eyes, and that smile. That perfect, beaming smile that could sear straight into your heart.

1987 was the most consequential year of his existence, and he remembered all of it. And most of all, he remembered her.

She was so—drawable. So, his pencil glided with ease, as if on autopilot.

He began by loosely moving the pencil around the sketchbook page until it began to form a rough shape, the outline of her sensational form.

With each pass of the pencil, he refined and perfected the shapes, using a kneaded eraser and a cotton swab to smudge when necessary, until he had her rough image down.

Then slowly, carefully using the appropriated pencil, stroke and pressure for each pass, he began to render in the details. Then, the shading, until—there she was—threatening to burst off of the page and into life.

It was Jennifer.

Rendered to perfection on the 12x9 piece of paper in front of him with such bold perfection, he was absolutely sure this was his greatest masterpiece.

He stared and dreamed. Then he stared and dreamed some more, feeling aroused by his drawing and the lost Goddess she represented.

He wanted her. He wanted her so bad, it was killing him. But more than that, he needed her. He needed her in the same way he needed to breathe air.

He needed her so bad it hurt.

Then, as he continued staring at the drawing, something happened.

At first, it was a strange sensation deep with him.

Next, he felt the sensation expand out all around him.

He could see, and he could feel something pulling at the sketchbook book page before him, lifting the graphite off the page and up into the air, into a moving, swarming, three-dimensional stream of pencil, ink, and shading.

It was the craziest thing he had ever seen—had ever experienced.

The traveling cyclone turned and moved and touched down onto the floor right in front of Jimmy as he stared with awestruck shock and wonder until he could see it right before him—see *her* right before him.

It was the drawing of Jennifer, but she was no longer in a static pose. She was animated with movement and form and precision and details to the minute for him to take in.

She was no longer just in black and white. As she continued to render and form and change, he could see she was no longer just a drawing or an animated drawing brought to life.

She was flesh and bone and matter and energy.

She was the essence of life itself as she took in a deep breath, opened her luminous, expressive brown eyes, and stared at the artist who had just created her by way of paper and pencil.

Jennifer was alive.

She was standing before him, and she was real. Very real. As real and as precious as anything he had had ever experienced before in his over five decades on this Earth.

At long last, Jimmy Barton had found a way to reach back in time to find his long-lost love.

Chapter 5 – For the World is Hollow, and I have touched the Sky

Jennifer was walking outside with her clipboard to get mileage readings on some trucks that had just been checked in.

One of these was the truck that Jimmy Barton was here to drive back to Pompano. So, she hurried the process and zipped through the paperwork at record speed to make sure it was she who was able to escort him to the waiting truck.

She thought about her philosophy class later today after she got off work at 2:30. She thought about fate versus destiny and what it all might have to do with how insanely drawn she was to Jimmy Barton.

She just needed to see him. Even if it was just a quick hello, or even a lingering stare or just a glance.

As she walked to the lot, she began to think about him in a dreamy kind of way, but in a way that was more intense than usual. It wasn't just that she needed her fix of him on the eye candy superficial level. That was pretty much true all the time; I mean, for God's sake, just look at him.

But now the way she was thinking, the way she was feeling was…different.

She began to intensely daydream about him, about actually being with him—physically—sexually—for real.

And as she finished getting the mileage reading from a truck, she climbed out of the truck, and there he was, standing before her like a dream come true.

They both smiled at each other, and she fumbled for words. She leaned in close to him to show him the clipboard and verify which truck he was taking back. Their hands touched, and it felt like an electric shock. She leaned in even closer, drinking in his smell and luxuriating in the touch of his hand and she turned to look at him, their faces only inches away from each other

And that's when it happened.

Jennifer felt the world around her spinning.

The sky seemed to open up, and she felt herself get pulled up into the brightest light she had ever seen.

For the world is hollow and I have touched the sky.

Then, everything changed.

She was standing somewhere in a house—in a kitchen next to a table by a set of sliding doors with a view of trees and a lake.

It was all so shocking. So surreal.

She had never been in this house or this kitchen before. Had never seen that backyard or that lake before.

But the man sitting at the kitchen table—holding a pencil and leaning over an open sketchbook as he stared at Jennifer, slack-jawed with the same look of confusion and awe that must have been on her face—he was familiar.

And the drawing on the sketchbook in front of the man—that more than just familiar. It was a drawing of her, rendered quite boldly with a spot-on likeness to her. She even recognized the outfit…and the pose. Both were from the company picnic this past June.

"Jennifer!" the man said, standing up, continuing to stare at her. But his look was different now. Confusion seemed to be giving way to sheer euphoric joy. And when she heard his voice and saw the way he was looking at her—that was when she knew.

She knew because that was the way she always dreamed he would look at her, outside of the rigidity of the workplace and unconstrained by his engagement to another.

The man before her was Jimmy Barton.

Yes, a time-warped future version of Jimmy Barton, as if he had gone through a six-hour makeup aging session done by one of those Hollywood special makeup effects gurus.

Yeah, he looked different and looked older, like maybe this was how his father or an uncle might look. But she knew this was not his father or an uncle. As insane and impossible and absolutely nuts as all of it was, she knew with every fiber, every cell, every fabric of her being, this was him. This was her crush. Her unrequited love. Her destiny. Her fate in Dr. Rhodes's philosophy class sense of the word.

"Jimmy," she said, staring into his eyes.

Sure, the hair was half gray and a lot thinner, long gone was that semi-afro of his. And the face had a few wrinkles. But the body was the same. Maybe bigger. Maybe even better. He certainly looked fit.

But the eyes that drew her in, as always, were exactly the same.

They both stood there, staring at each other until Jennifer did the very thing she had so urgently wanted to do from the moment she had first met him. She acted on impulse. She acted on passion and lust. She did the forbidden that she had always craved.

She kissed him. And he responded. Just as she always hoped he would. Just as she always knew he would.

It was the mother of all kisses—a soft, sensual, moist, soothing, caressing, insanely arousing, joining of lip and stroking tongue, as they held each other close, desperately touching, groping—wanting more and more.

This making out and touching and the groping went on for what felt like eternal bliss. Yet, it had to end eventually because there were things to talk about and questions to ask, and she could sense that he felt the same way too.

They sat down next to each other on a nearby couch, still maintaining a touch as if they both feared if they let go, all of this would end as quickly as it began.

"You're real," he said. "You're really here."

She looked at him, as unsure with her words as she was during those brief encounters at the South Shop branch and up at the Pompano office.

"I don't understand," she said. "How?"

"Jennifer, I don't know where to begin," he said, searching for the words.

She helped out by telling him what she had figured out already. This was the future. But it turned out there was more. More than she could have ever imagined in most wild Phillip K. Dick inspired philosophical ponderings.

"What do you mean by 'you drew me into existence'?" she asked.

"I know, it sounds beyond nuts. Fantastical. Impossible, and I don't understand it myself," he said.

"Maybe I should just show you," he said.

He stood up, offered his hand and led her across a dining room area, down a short hallway and into some kind of office that looked like a cross between a mini-art studio and the technicolor strewn bedroom of a teenager, complete with shelves lined up with action figures, books, and cases that had movie posters on them—like they were some kind of flattened or streamlined video cassettes, or maybe CDs with movies in them

The far wall was lined with a series of framed movie posters.

Some of them she knew, *Star Wars*, *Blade Runner*, and *Robocop,* a recent new movie in the theaters she had wanted to see. But there were others she had never seen before, including a colorful, bizarre image of a cartoon rabbit and a private detective called *Who Framed Roger Rabbit*, and something called *Pulp Fiction* with the image of a woman seductively lying on her stomach and reading a paperback book.

Visually, it was all too much to take in, and the sensory overload only added to her already jacked up, surreal state of disorienting, hyper euphoria.

Then, as Jimmy showed her a series of legal yellow pads with handwritten notes and paragraphs on them, things became even stranger.

The writing on the yellow pad looked like the rough draft or outline of something—of some kind of story. Then she read the words, and they jumped out at her—*Jennifer, South Shop, Traci, Mike Drithers, Dee, Dr. Rhodes, Jimmy Barton, crush, unrequited love.*

It was not just some story. It was her story. Her life. Everything, even her private thoughts and secret desires.

She was too shocked, too overwhelmed to speak at first. Then finally, she put down the yellow pads and tried to say something, but before she could, Jimmy had something else to show her.

It was a sketchbook. But not like the one back in the kitchen with the fully realized drawing of her. This was a rectangular book, and when Jimmy opened it, she recognized it as the kind of book animators and comic book artists used, because a friend of hers in high school aspired to be one.

But this sketchbook's content was not like any of the ones her friend had used. This one, like the handwritten notes and paragraphs on the yellow legal pads, was about her.

It was her life, down to the minute detail, laid out in a series of sequential pencil drawings as if Jimmy Barton—this Jimmy Barton standing next to her—had been there in the room jotting it all down like some kind of court reporter.

"I don't understand?" she said. "How? How can this be…How could you know all these things?"

She could tell he was as confused and bewildered as she was. But as he turned and looked at her, she sensed he was trying to reassure her. She felt his warmth. She could tell that this Jimmy Barton before her, regardless of who he was or how she came here, she could tell—she could feel—that he cared about her,

"Phillip K. Dick," she said.

His eyes lit up.

"Yes!" he said. "Yes. Phillip K. Dick. A universe within a universe. For the World is Hollow and I Have Touched the Sky. Yes. Yes, but I think that there is much more than that going on here. This is something else."

She looked at him and nodded, finding herself lost in his eyes.

"Yes," she said.

"Fate," she whispered. "Fate vs. destiny."

Chapter 6 – Jennifer's New World

It was like living inside a Phillip K. Dick book or short story—all of them at once.

Jennifer liked science fiction and loved philosophy and mind trippy stuff like movies from the late '60s and Pink Floyd's *Dark Side of the Moon*. But all of this—this sudden being whisked into a world that was on the one hand just the future year 2020, but on the other hand was more than that, since she was told she lived in a world *within this world*, that she was in fact from the scripted pages of a graphic novel being written and drawn by a future version of the hottie from work she had a crush on.

It was enough to make her certifiably insane. No wonder Phillip K. Dick was crazy if he sat around thinking about this shit.

"This is too much," Jennifer said.

"Yeah, tell me about it," Jimmy said.

"But I think I have a way for us to think about this," Jimmy said. "A way to make this easier for us to wrap our brains around. A way to process all of this. A way to figure out what to do next."

He had her attention.

Despite all the craziness, she felt something for him. Something more real than the giggly schoolgirl crush she had on him in her world. In the world of 1987.

"Instead of Phillip K. Dick and alternate realities, let's think of this as *Back to the Future*," he said. "Time travel by way of the sketchbook."

"So instead of a flux capacitor in a DeLorean like Doc Brown has, you have a sketchbook powered by your pencils," she said.

"And your imagination," she added.

"Yes!" he said. "Exactly!"

"But how did you know all these things in your writing and sketches?" she asked. "Stuff you were not there for. Even stuff in my head. My very thoughts."

"Maybe I just tapped into some universal zeitgeist," he said. "Or maybe it's because I think about you so much. I always did. Even back then."

"You did?" she asked.

"Yes, all the time," he said.

This made her feel good. Wonderful actually. To know that all this time, his feelings were not unrequited as she had feared.

"I think I literally drew you into the future," he said.

And what a future it was. 2020 was not what she would have ever expected. Not in a million years.

They were sitting in his office as Jennifer was recovering from being shown a handheld computer—an actual portable phone thing called an iPhone. As he showed her this device that looked like something straight out of *Star Trek*, Jimmy gave her the lowdown on the world of 2020.

Yikes.

A raging pandemic that was causing Jimmy (and everyone else) to quarantine. A country torn apart by an authoritarian vengeful sociopathic narcissist President whom she knew from 1987 as just some obnoxious, asshole, con man from New York. And to top it off, a video showing the police brutally torturing and executing a black man was setting off world-wide protests and even more division as the authoritarian leader dug in to create even more chaos and more division. Oh, yeah. And the Earth was on fire, literally, from something called climate change. Back in 1987, they called it global warming.

Double yikes.

"You got a lot of cool tech and nice gadgets. But really, this place is a nightmare," she said.

"Not exactly the bright future people would have imagined back in 1987," he said. "At least I know I wouldn't have."

This caught her attention and made her think about all the different variables that led to the future, not just for society, but for each individual. All of the decisions, from the epic and historical such as who is the President. To the minute and seemingly meaningless, such as what you have for breakfast or what time you get into the car to drive to work.

She thought about all the decisions she had made—and the ones she had yet to make. She thought about fate and destiny.

"Can I ask you something?" she said. "Something awkward and weird."

"Of course," he said.

"Did you ever wish…well, things had gone differently for you back then?" she said. "I mean, you know…between you and me?"

"Hell, yes," he said. "I mean here I am, a lifetime later, literally writing a book about that very subject. If only I had known the shit storm I was heading into with Phoebe. Well, I did know, deep down inside. I guess it was just easier to go along with it at the time."

"When did it end?" she asked.

"It never really began," he said. "But officially it was over by the summer of '88. Less than a year after I knew you…"

"What? So, you don't stay at Carlton?" she blurted out, suddenly panicked at the thought of her losing the only connection to him she had.

Then she added the next thought that popped into her mind, almost reflexively.

"Did you try to reach out to me?" she asked. "After it ended with Phoebe?"

"I didn't even know your last name," he said. "But I actually did call Traci to ask about you and…"

Just like that, he cut himself off.

"What?" Jennifer asked, standing there in a state of suspense and confusion.

"I don't think it's a good idea to say anymore," he said. "Knowing the future is…I wouldn't want to do that to you. The burden, I mean."

The look on his face…she could tell whatever he knew, it was not good.

"What is it? Something bad, right?" she asked. "Do I die or something? Am I still around now? In the world?"

"No, nothing like that," he said. "But now…I have no idea. I really don't know your last name, so I couldn't even Google you or look you up on Facebook."

"What's a Google? A Facebook?" she asked.

"Just a way of finding someone you lost touch with," he said. "Kinda like a universal phone book."

"It's Leski with an *I*," she said.

"Jennifer Leski," he said, looking at her in a way that was making her feel exactly the way she felt when he was near her in 1987. Dreamy and full of desire.

"So, can we do that thing now?" she asked.

"Huh?' he blushed. "You mean…"

"That Google thing," she said.

"Oh that," he said. "Well, I don't know, Jennifer. I still think that's a bad idea."

Then, before Jennifer could retort and plead her case, something began to happen to her.

Something bizarre.

She felt strange and surreal. Her very physical essence was changing. She felt and could see herself changing—her form altering from flesh and blood to shades of moving graphite, lines of pencil and shadow.

She was transforming into a drawing, just like the ones of her in Jimmy's sketchbook.

She cried out to him for help.

Jimmy desperately tried to hold on to her hand and keep her anchored into his world.

But three-dimensional flesh gave way to two-dimensional graphite.

Everything swirled around her into a tunnel that wrapped around her with dizzying darkness until she found herself right back where the whole bizarre episode had begun—in the South

Side parking lot of Carlton Truck Rental with Jimmy standing right in front of her. Their hands still touching.

She stood there for an eternal second.

Frozen. Unable to speak. Reeling.

"Jennifer?" Jimmy said. "Are you okay?"

Their hands were still touching. Jennifer didn't want to ever let go.

She wanted to tell him what had just happened. She wanted to tell him that she knew how he felt and that he needed to stop from making this huge mistake with Phoebe and that it would be a disaster and that it was fate and destiny that they should be together.

She wanted to say all these and more. But the sound of Dee's voice and the clicking of her boss's pumps moving across the asphalt jarred her out of her trance and dragged her back into this reality like a bucket of ice water.

It was something mundane and lame about giving Jimmy something to take back to Pompano with him.

The moment was lost and Jimmy soon departed. Jennifer went in to finish her workday and get ready for her classes as she thought about that world she had just visited. That future world with a future Jimmy Barton who had somehow managed to bring her there with a drawing.

It was beyond insane, and yet Jennifer knew it was all so very real. She needed to try and talk to Jimmy and make him understand. She needed to find a way to have time with him to do this. That would take some maneuvering. She needed a plan. In the meantime, she needed to talk to someone—someone who at least had a chance of being open-minded. She would try talking to Dr. Rhodes.

Jimmy stared at the drawing and concentrated as hard as he could.

He emptied his mind. He did deep yoga breathing. He concentrated on Jennifer, the very physical presence that had just been here in his house and in his arms only moments ago.

He thought about her curves and her eyes and her smile. He thought about her intoxicating smell and how insanely and sinfully erotic it was to kiss her—to be locked in that passionate embrace that spanned decades and world.

He thought about all these things with as much laser-like focus as he could muster. Then he waited and waited, but nothing was happening.

No matter what he did, it seemed he could not bring Jennifer back. And he wanted to so bad. He needed to so bad. He needed Jennifer in the way he needed air to breathe.

He went into his office and logged into the desktop. He Googled "self-hypnosis," thinking maybe if he put himself into a deep enough trance, it would increase the power of his focus and help will her back.

But none of the information seemed helpful. So he opened a new window for a new search, the one he had not been able to do before because he had not known Jennifer's last time.

He typed in "Jennifer Leski" and held his breath.

Of course, there were all sorts of people all over that place with the exact name. So, he sifted through all of the results, tried to get an image with the name and narrow it down to South Florida, and specifically Hollywood, where he knew she had lived. He did all this knowing full well that there were two other variables not accounted for as of yet—her married name if she had and if she had relocated.

Nothing. Not one match.

Next, he tried each of the social media sites, one by one, since most married women put their maiden names in there to make sure old high school friends can find them.

Still, nothing.

He thought for a moment and became overtaken with a sense of dread. What if…

He went into the Fort Lauderdale Sun-Sentinel section of old archived newspapers. He began to search through the local obituaries, issue by issue.

After what felt like endless hours, he finally got a partial hit. One for Estelle Leski.

Estelle Leski of Hollywood, Florida, died at the age of 47, and among those she was survived by was a 19-year-old daughter named Jennifer. The date of the entry was April 7, 1988.

The brief obituary did not mention anything about the cause of death. Jimmy got the feeling it was something brutal and unexpected. He didn't recall hearing anything about her having an ill mother, and she died so young.

He knew this was important, but not the big revelation he was looking for because the feeling of dread was still smothering him.

He kept clicking down and rolling forward in the obituaries but found nothing else. Then, just out of desperation, he just did a general local news search of the archives and what he got filled the entire screen.

It was a full article dated June 22nd, 1990 and the title said:

'Hollywood woman murdered.'

The article read.

"Responding to a 911 call about a report of a domestic disturbance, Hollywood Police were dispatched to the Regalwood Apartment Complex. Upon entering the apartment, they found the lifeless body of 20-year-old Jennifer Leski lying in a pool of blood. Michael Drithers, age 35, of Davie, has been arrested and charged with suspicion of murder. According to statements from nearby residents in the apartment complex, Mr. Drithers is Miss Leski's former fiancé. Beyond the police had no further comment other than to say the investigation is ongoing."

Jimmy sat at his desk for a moment, his head swirling in a storm of emotional shock. He tried to take a few deep breaths. To take it all in. To try and think clearly and plot his next move.

The whole Jennifer hooking up with Mike thing that Traci had relayed to him back in 1988 had made no sense. Why would a knockout sweetheart like her hook up with a dickhead like him? But he was known to be very manipulative and a shrewd operator. He must have played on her grief after her mother's passing. Used that to get in her good. She would have been vulnerable and felt obligated because he was "there for her."

Uggg! Fuck me!

Jimmy had to fix this. He had to find a way to warn Jennifer. He had to find a way to save her.

And he knew exactly what to do.

Jimmy looked at the yellow legal pad where he had handwritten the 1987 story treatment. He added everything that had just transpired—Jennifer being literally drawn into the future with him, the encounter, the kiss, the dialogue, and her sudden fading away. Then he opened the book of storyboard panels and began to sketch it all in frame by frame, working into the night until he had it all pretty close to fully rendered.

He fell asleep at his drawing board. Woke up at dawn. Had a cup of coffee, scarfed down a bowl of granola, then went right back at it. This time he began by drawing himself in the panels. His current self, being hand drawn back into the past, into the story, into Jennifer's world, just as she had been hand drawn into his.

He would be waiting for her on the North Dade Miami Community College campus when she walked out of the auditorium from her philosophy class with Dr. Rhodes. At least that was the way he was writing it and drawing it. Now, he needed to find a way to make it real. To sort of reverse engineer what he had done before.

He remembered his mindset at the precise moment Jennifer had materialized into his life. It was one of intense desire and desperate longing. It was a feeling of wanting and needing so bad it ached. He remembered how single minded he was as he stared at the drawing of Jennifer. How desperate his need for her was.

He gazed upon the newly created storyboard before him, intending to duplicate those feelings and that state of mind. He did not even have to try. So insanely urgent was his need to get back there and warn her about that murdering fuck Drithers, the desperation, the focus and the intensity came without an effort.

And as he stared at the storyboards, something began to happen.

He felt a tickling and then a pulling somewhere deep inside his core. The feeling grew and began to take over his entire body and mind like a wave of electrical shocks until—he felt himself begin to change.

Muscle, bone, and flesh gave way, transforming into a living, swirling graphite with shadow and substance as he felt his very essence being drawn—literally—down into and onto the storyboard page until—there he was.

In *1987*—both, the book that he had created, and in real 1987 too, at least as far as he could tell because he was no longer graphite and shadow, he was as real as the world around him. Which at this particular moment was the campus North Dade Community College, standing on a scenic sidewalk right outside the Conrad Hall lecture auditorium where he knew Jennifer was right now in her philosophy class with Dr. Rhodes. He knew because he had just written it that way only moments ago.

Then, a moment later, just as he had written as well, the class ended, and after the bulk of the students came swarming out of the building out onto the campus—there she was.

It was Jennifer.

This was as far as the scripted storyboard he was writing had gone. He had no idea what was about to happen next. He only knew he had to warn her about Drithers.

Jennifer was walking and talking with Dr. Rhodes as she walked out of the auditorium. This part, he did know because he had scripted it. She was trying to tell Dr. Rhodes about him—about Jimmy Barton and her experience of being transported into his world—of being literally hand drawn into the future.

He had no idea how Dr. Rhodes would react. He had not yet scripted that far. But judging by the look on his face, it was befuddled disbelief.

Dr. Rhodes scurried off, probably to teach his next class. Jennifer was alone now, so Jimmy stepped out from behind the park bench where he had been lurking and made his way toward her. Their gazes met. Her face lit up with exuberant joy.

Jennifer ran up and hugged him, holding him tight.

"I have no idea what happened. I tried to fight it and stay with you. I tried so hard," she said. "I never thought I'd see you again."

She stepped back, looking at him in a way no female had ever looked at him before. It made him feel all tingly in a way no other female had made him feel before.

"I mean, this version of you," she said.

"I was going to try and talk to you. The you that's here. To try and explain what happened," she said. "What I know. What I feel and the way that I know he feels, but is afraid to say or even to admit. If I told him what happened, he'd think I was crazy. But if he saw you. Then maybe he'd understand."

"Jennifer, I don't think we have enough time for all that," he said. "Whatever this transportation between worlds or times is, it seems to be like a burst of some kind of energy that burns itself out. Maybe a temporary state."

"Like a wormhole," he said. "A bridge that can't be maintained because of the energy required."

"So, you could vanish just like I did," she said. "And go back to the future. Any second."

"Yes," he said. "Which is why I need to tell you something. Something so important. And something that is not going to be easy for you to hear."

There was a tense and awkward moment of silence as Jimmy searched for the right words to say. But he could tell Jennifer was figuring it out.

"You were able to do that thing, weren't you? That thing on your computer and phone to search for me because you had my last name," she said. "And you found something out. Something terrible. I'm dead, aren't I?"

"Yes but, it will be okay now," he said, trying to keep her from getting too upset. "Because now I'm here and you can change all that. It's not random fate or destiny like you were learning about in Dr. Rhodes's philosophy class. The future is an outcome based on a series of decisions, some of which you can control."

For the first time, it just occurred to Jimmy that this was the theme of his graphic novel *1987*.

"But it's about destiny," she said. "And what if mine is to die, just like in that thing you read, no matter what we do to try and change it."

"It is about destiny," he said. "But you have something to say about that destiny."

He could see Jennifer's resolve strengthen right before his eyes.

"Okay then," she said with determination. "What do I need to do.?"

"First of all, avoid fucking Mike Dithers at all costs," he said.

"But I already try to do that now," she said.

"That changes in the very near future," he said. "You end up with him, and he murders you."

"What?"

She looked aghast—in shock.

"But that makes no sense," she said. "I can't stand the asshole. He's a creep, and I'd never let him touch me with a ten-foot pole."

"I know. But trust me, it changes," he said.

"But how?" she asked.

"He must manipulate you. Wear you down," he said. "Take advantage of a tragedy you will go through."

The horrific look returned to her face.

"What tragedy?" she asked.

As Jimmy went to answer, he felt it again.

The pulling. The start of the transformation. The swirling wormhole of graphite and shadow that connected his world to hers and the past to the future.

Fuck me. Not now!

Jennifer grabbed his hand, pleading for him to stay with her.

As he began to transform from flesh to graphite, Jimmy tried to shout to her above the cacophony of sound.

"It's your mother," he called out. "April 22nd, 1988. She passes away. Don't know the cause. Maybe sudden…Stay away from Drithers…"

His words echoed down into the swirling tunnel of graphite. He prayed they had reached her ears.

Chapter 8 – Do You Believe in Second Chances?

The tunnel of moving graphite and shadow flattened down onto the page, going from three dimensional to two dimensional, before Jimmy felt his ever-changing form bounce off the pages of the storyboard then out into the real world of 2020, as he morphed back into the living 3D solid matter flesh and bone.

He was in back his house, seated at the kitchen table, staring down at his storyboard sketchbook.

But something was different. The place felt...warmer. Not in the temperature sense. But in the emotional sense. In the living sense.

And it looked different.

The furniture. The layout. The design.

It had flair and color, and most of all, care. Like someone spent a lot of time planning and positioning every detail of the place. It was night and day compared to the sparse, cold, Spartan set-up he had before. He always had a clean and functional place. But it had been empty—emotionally and otherwise.

A graceful, sleek orange cat softly landed on the kitchen table next to his storyboard sketchbook. The wanting cat, meowed, then purred, winding around his hand and arm, craving affection. As the cat plopped down, Jimmy looked down at the sketchbook and could not believe what he saw.

These were boards he had never drawn before. Detailed sketches advancing the *1987* storyline far beyond where he had left off before plunging back into the past, and inside the book itself.

Now before him, laid out in glorious black and white with splashes of color and tint, was page after page showing Jennifer's actions and her life—after he had seen her on the college campus in 1987.

A storyline showing her using the knowledge Jimmy had brought back to her—avoiding the stalking, scheming Drithers— and even trying to figure out how to try and save her mother from whatever tragedy lay before her.

He immersed himself in the panels before him, devouring each drawing and advancement of the story as if he were being sucked into the most spellbinding graphic novel ever.

But before he could get to the good stuff, to see what happens with Jennifer and his young alter ego and Drithers and Jennifer's mother—he was interrupted by the sudden sound of the front door opening.

He could hear a dog panting enthusiastically, then around the corner, a gorgeous German Shepard came happily galloping up to him, wanting a proper greeting.

He could hear the sound of a dog leash being set down, the sound of breathing and soft footsteps. Then, the sound of a female voice that was as shocking as it was sweet—and familiar.

"You would have been so impressed, babe," she said. "Two miles, and we ran the bulk of it. Both of us. Well, it was more of a trot for him."

She came around the corner looking sweaty and hot, in every sense of that word, with a euphoric glow of exercised induced endorphins mixed with sun-kissed skin. She wore runner shorts and a t-shirt with artwork on it—the cover art of *1987* exactly as he had imagined it would be once he finished the book.

It was Jennifer. The Jennifer of his dreams and sketches. But also the real-life Jennifer.

She was older now, fifty, as she would have been if…

But there was no if anymore.

"Jennifer!" he said, drinking in her sight ever so carefully, just to make sure he wasn't dreaming or hallucinating or tripping out on some kind of creative binge.

He ran to her and hugged her, noting a wall full of family photos arranged in a collage on the wall behind her—photos of people he had yet to meet.

He kissed her. In very much the same way she had kissed him during that magical night she had first materialized straight out of the sketchbook and from the past into the present.

"It worked," he said.

At first, she seemed puzzled by his sudden burst of passion and by his words. But then he noticed her take in the book of storyboards behind them on the kitchen table, and he knew she understood.

"Dr. Rhodes, once he finally believed me about you, or at least I think he did—he said there would be a day like this," she said. "When you would remember."

"When the two timelines merged. When I returned to the new future that you created," he said.

She nodded and smiled.

"Well, someone once told me that I had the power to control my own destiny with the decisions that I made," she said. "So, I took that advice to heart."

She kissed him. Kissed him in a way that felt different and deeper and more sensual than any way he had ever been kissed before.

"But what decisions?" he asked a bit later after they spent some time following up that kiss.

"Really? You don't want me to ruin it with any spoilers, do you?" she said.

Then she went over to the bookshelf and pulled out a pristine, glossy thick graphic novel with the same artwork on the cover that had been on her t-shirt earlier.

1987.

She handed him the book.

"I think you're really going to like this," she said, smiling at him with a deep sense of satisfaction as if she too had been waiting for this moment forever.

"I already know one thing," he said. "I love the ending."